The
Ferry Port
Mystery

Introducing Irish detective Vikki Kirkby

David Pearson

Published by The Book Folks

London, 2023

ISBN 978-1-80462-132-5

www.thebookfolks.com

THE FERRY PORT MYSTERY is the first book in a series of standalone murder mysteries set on the south coast of Ireland. Details about the other books can be found at the end of this one, as well as info on David's other crime series, THE DUBLIN HOMICIDES and THE GALWAY HOMICIDES.

Prologue

"Come in, Inspector. Take a seat."

Superintendent Derek Harrington was a tall man. At fifty-six years old, he had worked his way up through the ranks, and had arrived at his elevated position by dint of hard work and an element of luck. He was known in the force as a fair person, but he could be quite severe too. DI Vikki Kirkby wasn't looking forward to their meeting. She knew it would be bad, but she had no idea just how bad it was going to get.

"Thank you, sir," she said, taking her place in front of the immaculate mahogany desk in the superintendent's office on the top floor of the Garda premises in Phoenix Park, Dublin.

"Now, Inspector," he said as she sat nervously before him, "I've studied this case very carefully, and I've spoken to your colleague, DI Jameson. It seems to me that there were some very serious mistakes made along the way, particularly with regard to the CCTV evidence that we didn't see fit to pass to the defence team in advance of the trial. That is, after all, what caused the trial to collapse, and earn us the scorn of the judge, is it not?"

Harrington sat back in his chair, his elbows resting on the desk, and made an apex with his fingers in front of his face.

"Yes, sir. But you should understand that I was not in charge of the case. DI Jameson was the SIO, and it was his responsibility to send that material to the defence lawyers, not mine."

"That's not what he says. He has told me that he specifically requested you to do that well before the trial. Do you not recall?"

"I don't recall, because it didn't happen, sir. Has the DI got an email, or a note, or any other evidence to support this assertion?"

Harrington put his arms back on the desk and leaned forward.

"Look, Vikki, there's a bit more to this than perhaps you realise. DI Jameson has had a long and very successful career with us. He's nearing retirement now, and he'll be gone in a couple of years. Furthermore, he has a wife and several children who are in college in Dublin. It would harm his reputation if he was to be found wanting as far as this case is concerned, and I don't want that. You, on the other hand, are young and bright. You'll have plenty of time to rebuild your reputation in the force after this, and if we can come to some agreement here today, I'll make sure your record is not negatively affected. But if you intend to slog it out against Jameson, I can imagine it might not end well for either of you. Now, what do you say?"

"What exactly have you got in mind for me, sir?"

"The commissioner has made it clear that heads have to roll. For the sake of the force's reputation, we can't just sweep it under the carpet. Don't forget, as a result of this bungling, a vicious criminal has walked free, albeit a certainty that we'll catch up with him at some stage in the future. So, you have a choice. You can either take a reduction in rank to detective sergeant, and stay on here in Dublin, although we'll probably have to move you to another station, or you can keep your rank and take a transfer to another division somewhere down the country. I believe you are originally from Wexford, isn't that right?"

"Yes, sir. But I left there years ago, and I don't really have any connections now in the place," Kirkby said.

"Yes, but it would make the story a lot easier to sell. We could say you had requested a transfer to be closer to your relatives now that they are becoming elderly. You know, that sort of thing."

"May I have some time to think about it, sir, and perhaps consult with my rep?"

"Eh, no. I'm sorry, that won't be possible. This thing is red hot just now, and I have to call the commissioner later and tell him how it has been resolved. He will be expecting me to have sorted it out, and to be honest, I don't think what I'm asking is unreasonable."

"I see," Kirkby said. Her stomach muscles tightened, and she wondered if she should tell this man to go to hell. But she quickly decided not to be seen to react emotionally, and after a tense moment, she simply said, "It seems that it's game, set and match."

"Does that mean you will accept a transfer to Wexford, then?"

"Yes, OK. But I need time to get things sorted out, and I want your assurance that whoever is in charge of my new station will not be expecting some dud who couldn't cut it in the Big Smoke. And I'll still be a DI?"

"Yes, of course, that goes without saying. The man in charge is Liam Frawley. I know him quite well, and I'll make sure he is properly briefed. You'll be working at the regional HQ in Wexford town. As to your need for some time to get organised, I propose a week's leave, starting today. Will that do it?"

"Yes, that should be fine. Thank you," Kirkby said.

"Very well. I'm glad we were able to sort things out. It's best for all concerned. Now perhaps you should go and clear your desk and hand over anything current before you leave."

"Yes, of course, sir. I hope we will have the opportunity to work together again some time."

Harrington got up and extended his hand. Vikki Kirkby shook it firmly, turned on her heels, and left the office. On the surface, she looked calm, if a little red about the face, but inside she was fuming. "How dare they!" she said to herself as she descended the stone staircase and left the building.

Chapter One

Wexford is a large town on the south-eastern corner of Ireland at the mouth of the river Slaney. It has a chequered history, dating back to AD 800 when it was first established by the Vikings. Later, it was taken over by the Norsemen, and then by the British, in whose hands it remained till the foundation of the Irish Free State in the early part of the twentieth century. Known for its benign climate and world-famous opera festival which takes place in the autumn annually, the area is also a tourist hotspot, as it features several wide sandy beaches.

DI Vikki Kirkby arrived in the town in late June. The town was both familiar to her and different at the same time. She hadn't been there for several years, but it was the area in which she had grown up before leaving to join the Gardaí against her parents' wishes. Her father had worked as the manager of one of the smaller branches of the National Bank in the town. Being a traditionalist, which largely accounted for her being christened Victoria, her father had assumed, wrongly, that his only daughter would follow him into that institution. But Kirkby had her mind made up that she wanted to join the Gardaí, so at the age of nineteen, she left the family home and enrolled in the Garda Training College in Templemore. Relations with her parents had been strained ever since, and only when her father was dying of lung cancer had she returned home, briefly, to help her mother through the ordeal.

On returning to her native patch, she had decided to avoid Wexford itself, and find a place well outside the town. She had located a rental on the web. It was close to Rosslare Strand, just a few minutes' walk to the expansive sandy beach, and close to the local Spar convenience store.

"It's a twenty-minute drive to the station, but if I'm going to be exiled in this place, I'm damn sure I'm going to stay somewhere decent," she had said to herself after she met the owner of the three-bedroomed detached house that would normally be a holiday let at this time of year.

Offering the landlord a full year's tenancy, he had reduced the rent from €700 a week to €1,200 a month for the whole year, and they had shaken hands. Now, with her Toyota Corolla stacked to the roof with most of her worldly belongings, she wondered if she had made the right choice. She might have been better living closer to the regional headquarters of the Gardaí in Wexford town centre. Time would tell.

Kirkby had been a rising star in the Dublin force. For the past year she had been working on a case involving the murder of a young woman. The victim's body had been found in a derelict house off Mountjoy Square several weeks after she had gone missing. Kirkby had worked the case with another DI for almost the entire time, collecting literally hundreds of witness statements, following up forensic leads, and finally arresting a thug who had apparently come across the girl when she was on her way home from the cinema late one night. He had raped and killed her. But her colleague was sloppy, and when the perpetrator was finally brought to court, the trial had collapsed. CCTV evidence upon which the prosecution was relying had not been furnished to the defence team, and as a consequence, the defence barrister basically drove a horse and four through the state's evidence, and the killer was acquitted with some harsh words from the judge about wasting his time directed at the Gardaí.

So, here she was back in Wexford. It wasn't fair, of course, but she knew that if she fought her corner up in Dublin, she would almost certainly come off second best. She would be the first female DI attached to Wexford's regional headquarters of the Gardaí, based off Mulgannon Road, close to the town centre. She hoped that the shenanigans that had seen her lose her post in Dublin hadn't preceded her arrival, but she had no way of knowing if that was the case. The fact that Superintendent Harrington knew her new boss didn't fill her with glee.

She pulled her car up in front of the house. She already had the keys, so she spent the next hour unloading all her clothes, kitchen equipment and foodstuffs, and arranging it as best she could in her new environment. When she had things more or less to her liking, she put the kettle on and made a cup of strong coffee. Sitting at the window in the kitchen-diner, the peace of the location with the bright blue sea clearly visible to the rear of the house began to calm her down, and she made her mind up at that point to make the very best of her new situation.

* * *

Kirkby arrived at the Wexford National Garda Headquarters at 8:30 in the morning. She had been advised to report to Detective Superintendent Liam Frawley who was in overall charge of the detectives at the station. She asked at the front desk for the man, and was told to wait. Several minutes later, a female officer in uniform came into the waiting area.

"DI Kirkby? I'm Garda O'Regan. The superintendent will see you now, if you'd like to follow me."

Kirkby fell in behind the uniformed officer and followed her down a long corridor. They got into the lift, and ascended silently to the third floor. A minute later,

O'Regan knocked on the door identified as the superintendent's office by the aluminium sign fixed to it.

"Come," boomed a voice from within.

Kirkby went in, and Garda O'Regan disappeared back the way she had come.

"Ah, DI Kirkby, I presume?"

"Yes, good morning, sir."

"Come in, come in. Sit down," the man said indicating a chair in front of his desk.

Frawley was a big man with a square face and silver hair that matched his pale, steel-grey eyes. Kirkby couldn't be sure from his accent, but he sounded if he hailed from somewhere north of Dublin, perhaps the north-west of the country.

"Can I get you a tea or a coffee, Inspector?"

"No thanks, sir, I'm fine."

Kirkby could see that the senior man was sizing her up. In her own estimation she was quite a good-looking woman. In her late thirties, she was tall and slim, with shoulder-length dark hair tied back in a ponytail, and a determined but pretty face.

"I've read your file, Vikki. As far as I'm concerned this is a new start for you. I haven't shared your situation with anybody here, but of course I can't guarantee that the grapevine isn't a bit ahead of us. You know what it's like. You'll find us a friendly bunch. It's not like the city. We still have our fair share of unpleasantness to deal with, but a good amount of our time is spent keeping the local lowlife in check, and of course we have the port to manage as well, although our colleagues in Rosslare handle all the routine stuff."

"May I ask who I will be working with, sir?" Kirkby asked.

"Yes, of course. We have four Dis and four uniformed inspectors here. Each of the Dis has a detective sergeant and there's a pool of detective Gardaí as well. You'll be one of the four from today. I'll take you down and introduce you to them in a few minutes," he said, looking at his watch. "Have you any questions for me, Vikki?"

"No, sir. Not now anyway. Oh, unless I'm taking over any active cases, of course?"

"I'll let your team fill you in on that. But there is just one other thing. It's a bit delicate, but it needs to be said," Frawley said.

"What's that, sir?"

"Well, it's just that you will be the first female DI here at the station. I know it shouldn't make any difference, but some people are not as quick to adapt as we would like, if you know what I mean. But if there's any nonsense, I want you to let me know immediately. I'll not stand for any misogyny on my force. Got it?"

Kirkby didn't like what she was hearing. In Dublin, female officers had been a fixture in the ranks for several years, and were now accepted and judged on their merits, at least by most. She had never experienced sexist remarks, and the closest she had come to having her gender recognised was when a junior Garda held a door open for her on one occasion.

"Yes, of course, sir."

"Right, well let's get downstairs and meet the team."

* * *

Kirkby thought she could detect some mutterings as she entered the open-plan area with the superintendent, but everyone hushed up pretty quickly when they came in.

"Listen up, everyone, I want to introduce DI Vikki Kirkby. DI Kirkby has been transferred from Dublin, and is a very experienced detective with a good track record." Some doubtful glances were exchanged between the group. Undeterred, Superintendent Frawley went on, "DS Waters, you'll be working with DI Kirkby. I'm sure you'll make her welcome. I'll leave you to get acquainted." With that, Frawley turned on his heels and left the room.

Kirkby regarded the detective sergeant. Waters was a portly young man with a ruddy face, badly dressed in an ill-fitting suit that was well worn, dirty black shoes, and a shirt that was in dire need of laundering. His tie, bearing evidence of previous meals, was loose around his collar and was clearly well overdue for the garbage bin.

"Well, Sergeant, perhaps you could show me to my office?" Kirkby said, looking at Waters and trying not to show her distaste of the man.

"Yes, of course, ma'am," Waters said, and gestured towards a corridor leading out of the open-plan office.

The office to which Kirkby was shown was an interior room with no window. There was a wooden desk, and on it was perched a PC, a phone, and a stack of three yellow stationery trays. A rather grubby chair was positioned behind it showing serious signs of wear. There were two additional visitors' chairs in the room facing the desk, and a grey steel filing cabinet to the left of the door. A single fluorescent tube, blinking above them, was the only source of light.

Kirkby placed her handbag on the desk, and went around to take a seat. She gestured to her colleague to do the same.

"OK, so let's get a few ground rules sorted out before we start," Kirkby said. "You can call me 'boss' or 'guv' if you insist, but not 'ma'am' – not ever. Got it?"

"Yes, boss," Waters replied.

"Good. Now, what have we on at the moment? Bring me up to speed," she said.

"There's nothing on our books at the minute, boss. It's a clean sheet," Waters said.

"So, what have you been doing for the last few weeks, then?"

"Waiting for you to arrive, boss," Waters said with a cheeky grin.

Kirkby sighed.

"Right. Well while we are waiting for the local scumbags to keep us busy, there's something you can do for me, Sergeant Waters."

"What's that, boss?"

"You can find me a proper office. This is a shithole, and I won't have it. OK?"

Waters made a face, and shuffled uncomfortably in his seat.

"Well?" she said, glaring at him.

He got the message, and prised himself up off the chair, scratched his greasy hair, and shuffled out of the room. Kirkby was beginning to have second thoughts already.

Chapter Two

Out in the open-plan, Detective Sergeant Cathal Waters was consulting one of the uniformed Gardaí about the request that had been given to him by his new boss.

"There's that office down in the corner with the big window overlooking the car park. It's full of junk just now, and it gets bloody cold, but it is a bit better than the one she's got. Give me an hour and Ciara and I will make it respectable. Will that do?"

"Sounds good, Joe. Thanks. I'll tell herself we'll have her sorted by lunchtime."

Waters left Joe O'Regan and Ciara Nestor to their appointed task, and as he was wandering back towards the inspector's current abode, having equipped himself with a coffee and a bun, he bumped into her coming the other way.

"Ciara and Joe are sorting out your office, boss. It should be ready by lunchtime," Waters said.

"Thanks, Cathal, I'd love a coffee. And if there's another bun to go with it, that would be even better," Kirkby said.

In fairness, she felt she might be overdoing the grumpy school mistress act a bit, which was not her usual demeanour, but she needed to assert her place as the woman in charge as soon as possible, even if it made her feel a little uncomfortable.

"You never get a second chance to make a first impression," her father had always said, and in this case, she reckoned it was very true indeed.

Kirkby perched on the edge of Cathal Waters' desk while he went to get her refreshments. He was back a minute later, armed with a cardboard cup of hot coffee and another bun.

"So, Cathal, tell me a bit about this beat. Who are the local mafia we have to look out for, and what sort of cases do you come across most often here?"

"It's a mixed bag, boss. A bit of theft from the shops in town. Some farm machinery stuff goes missing too – that's a bit more serious, cos that stuff costs a pile these days. Then there's some credit card fraud as well, and very occasionally, a violent crime to be dealt with – you know, fights on a Saturday night when the pubs close, and the occasional stabbing. But it's mostly small stuff."

"What about the locals?" Kirkby said.

"Ah, they're OK mostly. There's a bit of drink-driving, especially at the weekends, but uniform deal with that, unless there's car theft involved. There are a couple of families that like to test us occasionally, but we know who they are and they know the limit. It's not like the city here, boss. Everyone knows everyone else, and most of them know each other's business too."

"And what about the rest of my team. Who else have I got?" Kirkby said.

"It's just Terry Lucy at the minute, but he's out sick for a few weeks. He's from Cork, but he's OK to work with," Waters said.

"The superintendent said that there is a pool of detective Gardaí. How come you have just one?"

"We're a bit short-handed at the minute, boss. So, it's just me and Terry."

Kirkby was just finishing her coffee when the phone on Waters' desk rang. She picked it up before he could reach it.

"DI Kirkby."

"Oh, Inspector, sorry, I was looking for DS Waters."

"What for?"

"This is Sergeant Watkins from Duncannon. We've had a report of some kind of an incident out on the Hook Peninsula. I thought he might want to know about it."

"What sort of an incident, Sergeant?"

"Well, we don't know yet. I've sent two of the uniformed lads out in the car to see what's going on. They should be there in about fifteen minutes. Then we'll know more."

"OK. Well, where exactly is this then?"

"Out near Tobinstown, just short of Ramsgrange on the Arthurstown road. You turn down just after The Hollow Bar."

Kirkby was scribbling down directions as quickly as she could, but she wasn't keeping up.

"Hang on, Sergeant, I'll put you onto Detective Sergeant Waters. He probably knows the area."

Kirkby handed the receiver to Cathal Waters. He had been listening to Kirkby struggling with the directions, so he took the instrument with a slight smirk.

"Yes, Gerry," Waters said, "what's the story?"

Watkins gave Waters directions.

"Yes," he said, "I know the place. Just a few isolated bungalows down that road, if I remember it. We'll get out there now and see what's going on. Give me a call on the mobile if you find anything out while we're on the road. Thanks, Gerry."

Waters hung up the phone and looked at his new boss expectantly.

"Right, Cathal. We'll use your car as you seem to know the way. How long will it take us to get there?"

"Ah, about half an hour, I'd say."

"Right. Let's go."

* * *

Downstairs in the car park, Waters nodded towards a dirty blue Ford Focus that was parked facing the perimeter wall. He blipped the key fob, and the rear indicator lights flashed twice. Kirkby went to the front passenger door and opened it. Inside the car, the seat was covered in empty crisp packets and plastic wrappers from a couple of blueberry muffins. There was more rubbish in the footwell. Kirkby swept the crap off the seat onto the floor and stepped into the vehicle hoping that her clothes wouldn't get soiled by whatever else might be lurking on the upholstery. She closed the door and fastened her seat belt as Waters started the car and reversed out of the tight space.

"Cathal, if you're going to be working with me, you're going to have to clean up your act. This car is a health hazard."

"OK, but it's not a police vehicle. It's my own car."

"I don't care. If you are using it on Garda business, it needs to be respectable. Get it sorted."

"Yes, boss."

They drove on in silence out past Tracystown and Whitecross and through Wellingtonbridge towards Arthurstown. The roads were narrow, with high hedgerows on either side, and the atmosphere between the two officers in the car was decidedly frosty. When they passed The Hollow Bar, Waters slowed down, and a few metres further on, put out his left-hand indicator and turned down the L4045 into the townland known as Tobinstown. As they drove down the narrow road, they passed a few of the small, isolated cottages that Waters had mentioned before, until they came to a bungalow that had a Garda car adorned with colourful decals and topped with blue and red flashing lights parked outside, half up on the grassy verge. Waters pulled in behind it, and the two detectives got out.

The house that they were looking at was a small, single-storey building with a slate roof and fading white paint on its walls. The front door was positioned centrally, with windows on either side. The room to the left of the entrance had a large window, while the one at the other side was smaller. The front door was painted dark green, but the paint was cracked and peeling in places, and needed to be redone. There was a tiny garden in front of the house, comprised mostly of ragged grass that required cutting, and a narrow gravel path leading to the entrance that had weeds growing up through it. A uniformed Garda was stationed at the door.

"You don't want to be going in there, ma'am," he said as they approached, "it's not nice. Not nice at all."

Kirkby flinched at the use of the word. She noticed that the young officer was very pale.

"I'm afraid I have to go inside, Guard. It's my job. Now stand aside please."

Kirkby donned blue plastic overshoes and vinyl gloves and gently helped the young Garda to get out of her way by placing her gloved hand on his forearm. The officer stepped onto the overgrown grass, bent over forwards and vomited profusely onto the grass.

Inside the property the layout followed a familiar pattern. There was a small hallway with one room each to the left and right, and a narrow corridor leading to the rear where the kitchen or parlour was located, alongside another room which was presumably a bedroom. Kirkby noticed the acrid smell of gunpowder hanging in the still air. It was a distinctive smell that she recognised from other encounters with firearms, and it didn't bring back any happy memories.

As she advanced towards the kitchen, she spotted what looked like a twelve-bore shotgun discarded on the floor just at the entrance. Inside the kitchen, the customary scrubbed wooden table occupied the entire middle of the room. An old range sat against the far wall, still emitting some heat. Two worn armchairs were positioned on either side of the range, and in them were the corpses of a man and a woman. Each of them had suffered major wounds. The woman had hardly any face left, and much of her head was now spattered on the wall behind where she was seated. On the other side of the fireplace, the man appeared to have been shot in the chest. His shirt was torn and bloodstained, and his eyes, whilst still open, showed no signs of life.

Waters came into the room behind Kirkby.

"Jesus! What a mess," he said, stepping over the gun on the floor. "They're both dead, I presume?"

"Without doubt, Sergeant. What's your first impression?" Kirkby said.

"Hmm… looks like a murder-suicide to me, boss. The man probably shot the missus first and then blew himself away with the other barrel. What do you think?"

"I'm not sure. You may be right, of course. But how did the gun end up in that position if that's the case?"

"Recoil. If those aren't held tightly against your shoulder, the recoil is massive. It would have taken off across the room and landed here."

"I'm not completely convinced. We need forensics out to give the place a good going-over. Can you give them a call for me? And we'd better get the state pathologist on the job too. OK?" Kirkby said.

"If you say so, boss," Waters said, clearly wondering why she couldn't just accept the obvious.

"I want to see who found them and have a word. Come and find me when you've got the troops moving."

When Waters had gone outside, Kirkby walked slowly around the room, being careful where she placed her feet. Opposite the old range, an open-fronted dresser sat against the wall. Kirkby noticed a small pile of envelopes tucked in between a ghastly ceramic ornament of a bird of some kind and the side of the furniture. She went over and lifted out the papers. It appeared that the victims were a Mr and Mrs Roche. Opening one of the larger brown envelopes and removing the single sheet it contained, Kirkby saw that it was from Revenue and addressed to Mr Frank Roche, and it concerned his tax matters for the previous year. Another envelope with a handwritten address and an English stamp had been for Mrs Eileen Roche, and on inspecting the contents of that one, it appeared to be from the woman's sister, Maeve, who lived in Manchester.

Kirkby opened another door off the kitchen to reveal a bedroom that appeared to be where the Roches slept. It housed a double bed with dark brown head and footboards, neatly made up in an old pink candlewick bedspread. The floor was covered in an shabby carpet with a swirly green and brown pattern worn threadbare just inside the door. The other furniture comprised an enormous mahogany wardrobe with a mirrored front door and a drawer in its base, and a similarly styled dressing table, angled across the far corner of the room with three drawers and another, smaller, mirror on top. The room smelled musty and un-aired, and Kirkby observed that the small window looking out to the back garden with a net curtain across it didn't appear to have been opened in some time.

Chapter Three

Kirkby went back outside, keen to get away from the gory scene. The young Garda who had parted with his breakfast earlier had recovered somewhat and was looking a lot better. Kirkby went to speak to him.

"What's your name, Guard?"

"Dillon, Diarmuid Dillon, ma'am."

"Right, Diarmuid. Well, I'm Detective Inspector Kirkby. You can call me by name, or 'boss' but not 'ma'am' if you don't mind, I'm not the bloody queen! Now, do you know who found these people and when?"

"I'm not sure, m... eh, boss. We were out in the car and just got the call to attend."

"OK. Can you get back onto the station and see who called it in? Name and address would be good. Did you see anyone else here when you arrived?"

"No. The place was deserted except for... you know," Dillon said.

"How did you gain entry?"

"The door was open a bit. We knocked a few times, but when there was no reply, we just went in."

"And did you touch anything inside?" Kirkby asked.

"No, of course not. Well, maybe the door handles, but I didn't touch the weapon or anything."

"Is this your first violent death, Diarmuid?"

"Yes. I've been to a few fatal car accidents, but nothing like this."

"I know, it's very unpleasant. But you did well. Now, off you go and get me that information. And then I want you to put up some crime-scene tape all around. You do have some, I presume?"

"Eh, there might be some in the boot of the squad car. I'll go and have a look."

Vikki Kirkby wasn't used to this type of policing. In Dublin, everything would be underway by now. Forensics would be all over the place fingerprinting the house, examining the gun, and calculating angles and trajectories, while the pathologist would be making her own crucial observations. Here, it seemed like the pace was completely different. It would take her a little time to get used to country ways.

While she was waiting for Garda Dillon to come back to her, she went for a stroll around the outside of the

17

cottage. A side entrance led into a bigger patch of garden to the back of the little house. The grass in the back garden wasn't in any better condition than that in the front, but here there were some signs of industry. A large green metal garden shed that looked as if it had been recently painted stood at the end of the garden. As Kirkby walked towards it, she noticed that it had a very sturdy security lock across the two opening doors, and a powerful security light was mounted on the apex overhead. The security bar was held in place by two large ABUS locks, which Kirkby knew to be more or less tamper-proof.

Beyond the shed there was a wooden door set into the rear boundary wall of the premises, and Kirkby went to investigate. The door was locked and bolted, so she was unable to open it. But standing on an old milk crate, she managed to peer over the wall. Running along the back of the property there was a track, and parked upon it was a ten-year-old Peugeot Partner van with a Wexford registration and a slightly out of date tax disc. Kirkby took out her phone and photographed the vehicle, making sure to get the registration number in the picture, and then hopped down off the crate and returned to the front of the cottage.

* * *

Back at the front of the property, Diarmuid Dillon approached her.

"I checked with the call centre, Inspector. They didn't get the name or anything from the person that called this in. They said it was a woman who just said that something terrible had happened here. It was a very short call, and they said the woman was very distressed."

"OK, Diarmuid. Well, this is what I need you to arrange. Get back onto the call centre, and get them to find out what number the call was made from. Then get someone to do a reverse lookup on it to find the name and address, and bring it to me. You can get Detective Sergeant Waters to help you if you need. OK?"

"Yes, of course, Inspector."

Dillon walked off to find Waters looking a bit bemused.

God give me strength, Kirkby said to herself silently, this is going to be tough.

As she walked back out onto the road, her mobile phone began to ring. She looked at the screen but didn't recognise the number. She pressed 'answer'.

"Kirkby," she said to the instrument.

"Inspector, it's Superintendent Frawley. I hear you are attending a murder-suicide out in Tobinstown. Is everything OK?"

"Hello, Superintendent. Yes, we're just getting started out here, sir, but although it looks like murder-suicide, we'll have to wait till forensics get here and examine the scene, and the pathologist too, before we can confirm that."

"But what else could it be, Inspector? Two people found dead and a shotgun discharged and left nearby, I would have thought that it's obvious," Frawley said.

"Perhaps, sir. But I think we owe it to them both to be certain, don't you? The team will be here soon, and then we will know more. I'll keep you informed, sir."

"Very well. But I think you'll find I'm right, Inspector, and we have to be careful not to waste our resources chasing rainbows, and there's the poor people's family to consider too. Call me."

Kirkby was furious. She was now definitely of the opinion that she had made a mistake taking the posting in Wexford. She would have done better to take a drop in rank and stay in Dublin. She would eventually have got back to being a detective inspector, and she could have moved to another area in the city to start rebuilding her reputation after what had happened. But she was here now, and she had better make the best of it. She strode off looking for Cathal Waters.

She found him talking to Diarmuid Dillon leaning up against his car.

"Cathal, a word please," she said, interrupting the two men.

"I'm just sorting out this phone call thing with Diarmuid here, boss," Waters said. "We should have the caller identification in a few minutes."

"Yes, but I need to speak to you now please, Sergeant," she said turning her back and walking away.

Waters just shrugged and followed her. When they had gone out of earshot of the younger officer, Kirkby turned to Waters.

"Cathal, have you been speaking to Superintendent Frawley this morning?"

Waters looked down at his feet.

"Well?" she said, impatiently.

"He called me. He saw us leaving the station together and wanted to know where we had gone. I had to tell him."

"OK. Now what did you get from the call centre?"

"Diarmuid should have the caller's details by now. I'll check with him."

Waters walked back to where Diarmuid Dillon was standing.

"Did you get the information she's looking for, mate?"

"Sort of," Dillon replied, "the call came from a burner mobile. No trace of the caller's ID or anything, I'm afraid."

"Shit. She'll go mad!"

"It's hardly our fault. Anyway, why is she so determined to make something more out of this than the obvious?" Dillon said.

"Ah, who knows?" Waters said.

"Whatever," Dillon replied without conviction.

Chapter Four

The forensic team were the first to arrive. They had come across from Waterford, a distance of just forty kilometres, and were donning white paper suits and overshoes, getting ready to examine the scene. They would stay away from the bodies until the pathologist had examined them, but in the meantime, they started the laborious routine of fingerprinting the front door, the interior of the property and the surroundings. They lifted the shotgun up carefully and placed it in a large evidence bag. It would be taken back to the laboratory for examination, where better equipment and a sterile environment was available.

Soon after the forensic team had started their painstaking work, the large Toyota 4x4 carrying the state pathologist drew up on the now crowded road outside. Aileen Brophy alighted from the vehicle, and asked the uniformed Garda standing at the entrance to the house who the officer in charge was. The man identified Vikki Kirkby, bringing a smile to Brophy's face.

"Thanks, I know Vikki from before. I'll go and find her."

It didn't take long.

"Hi, Vikki. I didn't expect to find you out in the sticks. What's going on?" Brophy said.

"Oh hello, Doc. Nice to see a friendly face. It's a long story. I'll tell you again. Inside we have Mr and Mrs Roche, both deceased, apparently from gunshot wounds, but I'll let you determine the cause of death," Kirkby said, gesturing towards the front door of the house.

"Great! Any initial thoughts?" Brophy said, walking towards the entrance carrying a black attaché case full of instruments.

"It could be a murder-suicide. At least that's what my boss, Superintendent Frawley, thinks. But I'd welcome your opinion," Kirkby said.

"OK, let's get started then."

Inside the kitchen, Brophy began by walking around the bloody scene, observing. When she had reviewed the spectacle before her thoroughly, and spoken notes into her pocket recorder, she moved in closer to the bodies. She examined Mrs Roche first. She leaned in close to the dead woman's head. She took out a small, illuminated magnifying glass, and studied the woman's upper body carefully, whispering notes into the recording device. After a few minutes, she moved across to the dead man. Again, she leaned in with her magnifying glass and studied the corpse carefully. After a few minutes, she stood up and stepped back, away from the bodies. She turned to Kirkby who was standing in the doorway.

"This isn't murder-suicide, Vikki. No way."

"Oh. How come?"

"It's obvious if you look at it carefully", Brophy said. "Firstly, if it was, are we supposed to believe that Mr Roche shot his wife from a standing position in front of her, and then calmly sat down in the other chair and blew himself away? Very unlikely."

"And…?" Kirkby asked, sensing that there was more to come.

"And, in any case, they were both shot from a distance of at least two metres or two and a half. There are no powder marks on either of them, and there would be if the man had shot himself. And, additionally, it's almost impossible to shoot yourself in the chest with a full-length shotgun, especially from a sitting position. Where was the gun found?"

"By the door, on the ground," Kirkby said.

"There ya go! Have forensics got it?"

"Yes, they're taking it away for examination."

"Good. Get them to look for fingerprints other than those of the deceased, and specifically on the cartridge cases. Was the gun broken?" Brophy asked.

"No, I don't think so."

"Good. But I'd say you have a double murder on your hands, Vikki. Sorry."

Kirkby went back outside to find DS Waters. She was glad to get away from the horrendous scene inside the house in any case.

"Cathal, the pathologist has said that this is not a murder-suicide. It looks as if these two were deliberately killed. So, we need to get busy. Can you get back onto the station and see who is available to start digging?"

"Yes, OK, boss. What are we looking for?"

"As much as we can get. Next of kin. Where the Roches were employed. Did Frank have a shotgun license? You know, all that kind of stuff and anything else that occurs. And don't hang about. This is urgent!"

Waters didn't give the appearance of a man in a hurry, but he went back to his car, sat inside, and called back to the regional headquarters in Wexford.

Kirkby then approached the lead forensic officer dressed in a white paper scene-of-crime suit who was dusting the front door for prints.

"Hi. The pathologist has just told me that she thinks these two were murdered. Can you see if you can find any evidence of forced entry anywhere?" she said.

"Yes, sure. But I bet you most of the folks around here aren't too fussy about keeping their places locked up when they are inside. It's not a big crime area after all," the man said.

"Tell that to the two victims inside. Any useful prints?"

"Yeah, lots. We'll have to sort them out later on. I'll let you know."

As Kirkby was wondering what to do next, an elderly man dressed in a waxed jacket and with a brown check cap on his head accompanied by a black and white sheepdog came strolling along the road. As he approached Kirkby, he asked, "What's going on here?"

The dog was frisky, and went right up to Kirkby wagging its tail furiously, and trying to lick her hand.

"May I ask your name, sir?"

"Talbot, Michael Talbot. Why? Who are you?"

Kirkby introduced herself holding up her warrant card.

"Do you know the occupants of this property, Mr Talbot?"

"Yes, of course. It's Frank and Eileen. Why? What's happened?" Talbot said.

"That would be Frank and Eileen Roche?"

"Yes, of course, didn't I say. Are they OK?"

"I'm afraid there's been a violent incident here at the house, Mr Talbot. Mr and Mrs Roche have been killed. How do you know them?"

"Killed! That's crazy. God, I only saw the pair of them yesterday evening. Are you sure, officer?"

"Yes, I'm afraid so. How did you say you knew them?"

"I live in the next house along the road, around the corner. We're neighbours," the man said. He had gone quite pale.

"And what time last evening did you see the couple?"

"Eh, let me see, it would have been about eight or a quarter past. They were out for a walk and passed my place. I was in the garden, and we exchanged greetings. They were both fine then. What happened to them?"

The dog had laid down on the warm tarmac with its head between its front paws, keeping a careful eye on proceedings.

"What was Mr Roche's occupation, Mr Talbot?"

"He works at the port in Rosslare for one of the ferry companies. I think he might be involved in loading and unloading the ships, or something. He'd been there for ages."

"Did Mrs Roche work?"

"Yes. She's part-time at the school over near Wellingtonbridge. I'm not sure exactly what her duties are."

"Mr Talbot, after you had seen the Roches last night, did you see or hear anything unusual later on? Any strange vehicles passing on the road, or any loud noises?" Kirkby said.

"No, I can't say I noticed anything out of the ordinary. Can I ask you what exactly happened to them, Inspector?"

"Our investigation is just starting, Mr Talbot. We'll know more later on today. Did the Roches have any children?"

"Yes, they did. Just one boy, although he's grown up now, obviously. He works in Customs and Excise in the port in Cork, but he visits his parents quite often."

"I don't suppose you have a contact number for him?"

"No, but if you call Cork Customs, they'll be able to put you in touch."

"What's his name, the son, I mean?"

"Daniel. They call him Danny."

"Right, thanks, Mr Talbot. That's been very helpful."

"What happens now?" Talbot said.

"The bodies will be removed to Waterford shortly for post-mortems. And our forensic people will be here for the rest of the day, and maybe tomorrow. Then it depends on where the investigation leads us."

"Do you think this was a random thing, Inspector? Should we be concerned for our safety around here?"

"It's too soon to tell, but apart from the usual precautions of locking your house up securely when you go out, and at night, I don't think you need be overly concerned. These things are seldom random."

"Oh, OK. Well, I'd better let you get on. C'mon, Shep, let's go."

The dog eased itself up from the road and jogged along beside its master, sniffing the verges as the two of them disappeared down the road and around the corner, out of sight.

Chapter Five

Cathal Waters came back to the front of the house where Kirkby was sitting waiting for the pathologist to finish up, and have the bodies removed in the black Mercedes van that had arrived a short time earlier.

"Well, Cathal, what's the story?" she said.

"I've been on to the station. The lads in Cork are going to get in touch with the son and break the news to him. The boss says we can have a couple more uniformed officers out here to do a house-to-house if you want to, but I sensed he wasn't best pleased."

"OK. Well, I'll deal with that. As soon as the bodies have been removed, I want you and I to give this place a good going-over. There may be something in the house that will give us a clue as to what caused this."

Waters looked a bit disgruntled, but decided not to make an issue of it for now at least.

As they were finishing the conversation, Kirkby's phone rang.

"Kirkby."

"Hello, Vikki. It's Superintendent Frawley here again. Your sergeant has told me that you think the Roches were murdered, is that right?"

"It's not me saying that, sir, the pathologist has expressed that view and has given me the rationale, but of course they'll know more when a post-mortem has been performed."

"I see. But are we sure this couldn't just be put down to two elderly people leaving the planet together due to some terminal illness, or something? A double murder is extremely unusual around here, and more than a little inconvenient."

Kirkby could feel the blood rising in her face.

"Well, if you're ordering me to treat it so, then very well, that's what I'll do. But I'll have to record my own views on the matter and how it came about that we decided not to investigate a serious crime. And there's still a murderer on the loose too."

"Inspector Kirkby, I don't like being threatened!"

"Me neither. Now, are you going to let me get on with my job, sir?"

Frawley said nothing for a few moments.

"Are you sure you're up to it? Would you not prefer if I got someone else to handle it, given what happened in Dublin?"

It was Kirkby's turn to remain silent for a moment so that her anger didn't overwhelm her.

"I think you'll find that I'm well able to manage, sir, given the right resources and the support of the rest of the team. I will, of course, keep you informed of our progress." She cut the call off before she said something that she would later regret.

When she had cooled down, though not totally, she went in search of Cathal Waters.

"Cathal, I need a word."

The two of them went back out onto the road where they could not be overheard.

"Cathal, what did you say to Frawley?"

"Nothing, boss."

"Look, Cathal, I need you to be truthful here, so, what did you say to him?"

"When I rang the station, there was a message for me to call him. He asked me what the story was and how you were handling it. I told him that it looked to me like a murder-suicide, but that you had other ideas. He told me to say nothing to you about the call."

"Terrific. Well, I've just had a nice earbashing from him thanks to you. Now we need to get something straight,

Cathal. If you ever go behind my back again, ever, it won't end well for you. Got it?"

"Yes, boss. I'm sorry."

"Listen, Cathal. I don't think you've really got the idea of teamwork yet. If you and I are going to work together, there may be times when we get into some difficult scrapes. One or both of our lives may depend on the other covering our backs. You might think these things can't happen in a backwater like this. But trust me, it can. And it can happen very unexpectedly, and very quickly. So, you're either with me, or not. Which is it going to be?"

"I'm with you, boss," he said rather unconvincingly, refusing to make eye contact.

"Right, I should hope so. And that means that we manage the message upwards and outwards too. Understand?"

"Yes, boss. Totally."

"Good. Are you firearms-trained?"

"Yes. They sent me on the course last year, but I've never drawn a weapon on duty," Waters said.

"Well, let's hope you don't have to, but it's good to know. If my instincts are correct – and they usually are, by the way, despite what you might have heard – we could be dealing with some pretty ruthless types here. So be prepared for anything. Now, let's get in there and see what we can find," she said, nodding towards the house.

* * *

The bodies of Frank and Eileen Roche were lifted carefully from the positions in which they had been found, and placed into thick, rubber body bags and zipped up. Then each in turn was placed onto a narrow trolley and wheeled outside and put into the black van. When they were safely inside and secured, the vehicle took off at a sedate pace towards Waterford. Aileen Brophy was coming out of the house, removing her protective clothing, as Kirkby and Waters approached.

"Finished, Aileen?" Kirkby asked.

"Yes, for now at least. We've taken lots of photographs and samples from around the bodies. The forensic lads will be here for a while yet collecting evidence. I'll try and get Waterford to do the post-mortem later on, but it depends how busy they are."

"Anything you can tell me now, like the approximate time of death?"

"Don't quote me on this, Vikki, but I'd say between nine and midnight last night. I can probably narrow it down a bit when the PM is complete."

"Who is the contact in Waterford?" Kirkby asked.

"It's a Dr Bukowski. He's Polish. We're lucky to have him. I've worked with him before. He's excellent. A bit intense, but a damn fine medic."

"Great. Thanks. I'll see you anon then. Thanks for your help."

"No problem, Vikki, and good luck with it," Brophy said and walked off towards her own vehicle to drive back to Dublin.

"You take the bedroom, Cathal. And I want a thorough search: under the mattress; behind the drawers; on top of anything tall, and lift the edges of the carpet too in case there are loose floorboards. If you find anything significant, give me a shout, OK? I'll be in the kitchen-living room."

"Yes, boss," Waters said, but Kirkby wasn't entirely convinced that his heart was in it.

She called after him. "Oh, and get those other two uniformed officers out here as well to do a house-to-house."

"Righto," he muttered as he disappeared into the room.

Kirkby started to search the kitchen thoroughly. She looked among all the utensils, pots and pans, cutlery and dry food stored high up in the cupboards, but found nothing of interest – just some obvious mouse droppings. Then she went to the dresser and opened the lower part which had two hinged doors that met in the middle. The dresser was painted green and cream, and looked to be straight out of the 1950s. Within it were two shelves. On the upper shelf she found a metal biscuit tin which she removed and rested on the shelf halfway up the piece of furniture. Inside the tin were papers of all kinds. Old bills and receipts, a few letters, two passports that were both out of date, and a passbook for the local Credit Union. She opened it up, and found to her amazement that it showed a sum of €45,000 in credit. Lodgements to the joint account had been sporadic rather than regular, but came in amounts of several hundreds, with occasional deposits of over €1,000. There were some regular withdrawals too, again mostly €1,000 a time, and one that was made the previous Christmas to the tune of €2,500.

Kirkby put the entire tin and its contents into a large brown evidence bag, sealed it, and wrote on the label. Then she went outside to put the bag into the boot of her car. As she closed the boot, a Hyundai Garda car pulled up outside. Joe O'Regan and Ciara Nestor got out of the car and walked over to the inspector.

"Hello, Joe, and you must be Ciara. I'm Inspector Kirkby. I'd like you to start doing door-to-door enquiries around here for me. See if anyone heard or saw anything out of the ordinary last night, or if anyone heard any loud bangs. Cover all the properties in the area, and if anywhere there is no reply, leave a note for the occupier to contact us on their return. OK?"

"Yes, boss," Ciara Nestor said, removing a notebook and pen from her uniform pocket.

"I'm going back to the station. I want to get some enquiries started there. Can you report your findings to DS Waters when you've finished? Right, off you go."

Before she left the murder scene, Kirkby spoke to Waters and told him about the work the two uniformed officers had been told to do, and that they would come looking for him when they were done.

"I'm heading back to town, Cathal. But while I'm gone, see if you can get into that shed in the garden. There might be something interesting inside."

"OK, boss," Waters said.

"And if you find anything unusual, call me. In fact, call me anyway when you get into it."

"Right, boss."

Chapter Six

Back at the Garda station, Kirkby went to her office. She needed more manpower but wasn't sure how to go about getting it. She didn't want to ask Superintendent Frawley in case it would be seen as a sign of weakness on her part. But she knew she couldn't hope to bring the killer to justice without more help. She was trying to figure out what to do when a man knocked on her door.

"You must be the new DI down from Dublin. I'm Jim Kennedy. I was out earlier when Frawley was introducing you. I'm one of the other DIs."

"Hello, Jim. I'm Vikki Kirkby. Come in. Grab a seat."

Kennedy was tall, with a trim figure and salt-and-pepper hair, and was dressed smartly in a grey suit with well-polished shoes and a pale-blue shirt with a button-down collar. Kirkby was relieved to see that not all the detectives in the station were as slovenly as her sergeant.

"How are you settling in, Vikki?"

"Getting off to a bit of a shaky start, to be honest. Looks like we have a double murder out near Tobinstown. A couple; Frank and Eileen Roche. Apparently murdered in cold blood with a double-barrelled shotgun."

"Cripes! You do have your hands full."

"Yes, and I'm going to need some more detectives. One of my team, Terry Lucy, is out sick, so I'm already short-handed. I don't suppose you have anyone you could spare?" Kirkby said.

"Sorry, my team are fully deployed just now. But have you met Ciara Nestor? She's one of the uniformed Gardaí here," Kennedy said.

"Yes, I have. In fact, she's out at the site now doing door-to-doors with Joe O'Regan. Why?"

"Well, she's a bright girl, and I know she wants to be a detective. Maybe you could co-opt her for the duration of the investigation. Try her powers of detection out, as it were. I can square it with Frawley if you like?"

"Would you? I'm not his favourite person just now," Kirkby said.

"Ah, don't mind him. He's OK really. He'll come around once you have a few wins under your belt, don't worry. Well, look, I'd best get on. I'll catch you later, and I'll talk to Frawley," Kennedy said.

"Right, thanks. But just before you go, is there anyone around here that does technology?"

"Well, we don't have a technical bureau as such, but there's a guy on the floor beneath us that loves all that stuff. He's a real nerd, but a nice fella too. Conor Grogan is his name. He'll give you a hand with a phone or a PC or whatever. Now, I really must be off."

"Yes, sorry, of course, and thanks, Jim."

Kirkby was about to go in search of Conor Grogan when her mobile phone rang.

"DI Kirkby."

"Hello, boss. It's me, DS Waters. I managed to get into that shed in the back garden out here. I couldn't find the keys anywhere, but I used a wrecking bar I keep in the boot of my car and I was able to remove the hasp that was keeping it secure."

"Yes, well done, Cathal, but what did you find inside?" Kirkby said, becoming a little impatient with her sergeant's meandering style but trying not to show it.

"That's the funny thing. Inside there are several racks of plastic shelving. It's arranged all along the three interior walls. And on each shelving unit, there are cardboard boxes full of documents. There must be nearly a hundred boxes in all, maybe even more. I had a look inside one or two of them, and they seem to be customs documents of some sort."

"Right, well can you arrange to have some of those boxes collected and brought back in here as soon as possible?"

"How am I going to do that, boss? There are loads of them."

Kirkby's patience was running out.

"Jesus, Cathal. Get onto transport and get them to organise a bloody van, or something. It can't be that hard!"

"Oh, right, yes, boss."

"And have the other two finished the door-to-door enquiries yet?" Kirkby said.

"I don't know. I haven't seen them for a while."

"Right, well never mind that. Focus on the stuff in the shed. And before forensics leave, get them to look for any evidence of a vehicle at the front of the house. Whoever did this hardly walked to the place."

"OK, boss. I'll talk to them now. They're nearly done," Waters said.

"And when you see Ciara Nestor, could you ask her to call me please?"

"OK, boss. Bye."

Kirkby was beginning to think that Waters was a bit of a dead beat. It was hardly surprising that she had been lumbered with the least effective officer in the station. But there was no point in making a fuss about it at this early stage. She'd have to see if she could mould him into some sort of shape, but it wasn't going to be easy.

* * *

Garda Conor Grogan was much as Inspector Kennedy had described. He had a youthful appearance about the face, but he was tall and slim with his hair cut short, and he sat at a desk festooned with a number of mobile phones and laptop computers, with their associated collection of cables, chargers and USB memory sticks. There were a couple of other sophisticated-looking gadgets that Kirkby didn't recognise as well.

"Hello," she said, approaching his desk, "you must be Conor. I'm DI Kirkby." She extended her hand, which the young man took and shook firmly.

"Nice to meet you, Inspector. How can I help you?"

Kirkby told the young man about the murder out at Tobinstown.

"Would you be the right man to look into the victims' background, you know, their bank accounts, social welfare stuff and mobile phones?"

"I could do. Is it urgent?" Grogan said gesturing towards his obviously busy desk.

"Well, kind of, if you can handle it. We didn't find any mobile phones, but I imagine at least one of the victims must have had one. And I'd like to have access to their financial records. I know they had a Credit Union account, for example, but they must have had bank accounts too."

"What else do you know about them, Inspector?" Grogan said.

"The man worked at the port in Rosslare for one of the ferry companies, I think, and the missus was a part-time teacher in Wellingtonbridge."

"That makes it easier. Sure, I'll have a go for you. Will it be OK if I start first thing tomorrow? I'm a bit backed up today."

"Yes. Thanks, Conor. That'll be fine. I'll drop down a biscuit tin full of papers I found out at the house to help you get started."

"Great, thanks."

Kirkby went upstairs and retrieved the old biscuit tin, bringing it back down to Grogan.

"Thanks, Inspector. Has this thing been dusted for prints or anything?"

"Oh, shit, no, it hasn't. But I don't think it was handled by the killers. I found it in the bottom of a dresser. It didn't look to have been disturbed, and in any case if there was robbery involved, they would have taken the Credit Union passbook. But thanks, give it the once over just to be sure."

"OK, I'll do that before I handle it, and put the results into PULSE in case there's a match."

"Thanks, Conor. I'll give you a call tomorrow afternoon then."

"That's a bit more like it," she said to herself as she went back upstairs.

* * *

It was late afternoon when Kirkby got back to her office. There was a voicemail on her desk phone from Ciara Nestor.

"Hello, Inspector. You asked me to call you. If you need me, you can get me on 084 788 6227 anytime. Thanks."

Kirkby dialled the number. It was answered almost immediately.

"Hi, Ciara. Thanks for ringing in earlier. How did the door-to-door go with Joe?"

"Sorry, boss. Nothing doing. That place is pretty remote. We did speak to a few neighbours, but no one said they saw or heard anything out of the ordinary."

"Hmm, right. Look, I was wondering if we could meet for a quick chat later on."

"Yes, of course. I can come back to the station now. I'll be there in half an hour."

"No, I'd prefer to meet off the premises. Where do you live, Ciara?"

"I live at home out near Tagoat."

"Excellent. I'm staying in Rosslare Strand myself. Why don't we meet at the Hotel Rosslare at seven o'clock. If you haven't time to eat, we can get something there. Is that OK?" Kirkby said.

"Yes, of course. I'll see you there then," Nestor said.

Nestor was clearly curious about the phone call with Kirkby. Why did the inspector want to meet her away from the office? What was on her mind, or was there something personal to it? She couldn't figure it out, but she was determined to go ahead with the meeting and see where it led.

Chapter Seven

The Hotel Rosslare is situated on high ground directly overlooking the ferry port in Rosslare Harbour. It's a busy place, with ships coming and going most of the time throughout the day. The main routes used to be to the UK, where Irish Ferries operated to and from Pembroke Dock in South Wales, along with Stena Line going to Fishguard on the old British Rail route. But more latterly, services between Rosslare and the Continent had been introduced, and there were now several services to northern France, and even a sailing twice weekly to Bilbao in northern Spain.

The hotel accommodated many of the passengers who arrived in the port during the night or late evening, and were too weary to continue their journeys. There was also quite an amount of local trade that kept the bar in the hotel busy, and a sprinkling of Irish tourists too, enjoying the pleasant climate of the 'sunny south-east' as it was called, as well as the excellent food served in the hotel restaurant.

Kirkby was seated in the foyer nursing a small glass of cold white wine when Ciara Nestor arrived just after seven o'clock. She had, mercifully, stopped off at home to change out of her uniform and was now casually dressed in nicely fitted blue denim jeans and a pale blue, sleeveless, polo shirt. Her dark blonde hair, usually tied into a tight scraped-back ponytail for work, hung loosely around her shoulders.

"Hi, Ciara," Kirkby said, standing up, "can I get you something to drink?"

"Hello, boss. Yes, please. May I have a beer? I'm not driving. My dad dropped me over, and I'm hoping you'll give me a lift home when we're done."

"Yes, of course."

Kirkby went to the bar and got a cold bottle of Heineken and a glass, and brought it back to where Nestor was seated, looking slightly apprehensive.

Nestor poured the drink into the glass, took a sip, and said, "Well, Inspector, may I ask what's on your mind?"

"Yes, of course. Sorry about the secrecy, but I didn't want to discuss things in the office. Walls have ears, and all that. Oh, and by the way, it's Vikki when we're off duty."

Nestor smiled, and took another sip of her beer.

"I wanted to ask you if you'd be interested in joining my team as a detective, Ciara. You've been recommended to me by another senior officer, and I'm desperately short-handed on this case. I need more help, and I'm not confident the superintendent will give me the best available personnel."

"Wow! That's a lot to take in at the end of a shift. Can I ask if you have told the super, or if he knows?" Nestor said.

"That's being taken care of. I can't make it official just yet, because you'll need to do the detective training in Templemore, but there's nothing to say a uniformed officer can't be co-opted as a detective temporarily. What do you think?"

"I think I'd like the challenge, but I'd be concerned what Joe and the others would think. They might be very put out that one of them wasn't chosen."

"I know what you mean, but the thing is I need to know if you're up for it pretty soon. This Roche case may be quite complex, and I need help with it. So can you have a good hard think about it and let me know as soon as possible. And please don't discuss it at the nick, for obvious reasons."

"Yes, OK, bo… eh, Vikki. But there's something else that you might need to be aware of, given we're talking confidentially," Nestor said, avoiding eye contact with Kirkby.

"Oh? What's that?"

"It's a bit tricky, but here goes. The week before you came down here, we were out at the pub on the Friday. Frawley was there, and a good few of the senior officers, as well as Sergeant Waters and a few of us too. Frawley got a bit pissed, and he started slagging you off. It was pretty nasty, so much so that Inspector Kennedy took him aside and had a word. Frawley left soon afterwards."

"I see. I knew he wasn't very pleased at my arrival on the patch, but I didn't think it was that bad. I won't embarrass you by asking what was said."

"Thanks. To be honest, Frawley has a bit of a reputation. If he doesn't like an officer, he can make life hell for them. We've lost a few decent cops as a result of his crap, who left under transfer to other regions."

"Terrific! But tell me, what's Kennedy like?"

"Jim's great. He's a sweetheart. Don't get me wrong, he can be as tough as nails when the occasion demands, but he'd walk on hot coals for any of his team, and vice versa," Nestor said.

"Hmm… I thought as much. He stopped by to see me, and it is him who is arranging for you to be in your own clothes with Frawley – that's if you're up for it."

"I'll definitely give it some thought. Was there anything else, Vikki?"

"No, nothing else. Thanks for coming out. Finish your drink and I'll drop you home."

As Kirkby drove away from the hotel, out past Kilrane towards Tagoat, Nestor asked, "Do you know the area at all, Vikki?"

"Oh, yes, I'm a bit rusty, but I'm re-acquainting myself with the place. I was born and reared in Wexford. My father was a manager at the National Bank on the Crescent, and I lived at home till I was nineteen and ran away to join the circus, as it were. Have you lived here all your life too?" Kirkby said.

"Yes. My folks do a bit of farming, and my dad is a part-time builder. Nothing major, just the odd house extension or garage, that sort of thing. What school did you go to? It's the next left, just here."

"I went to Selskar in town, or as we used to call it, 'Selscab'. It wasn't bad actually. My parents thought it best to send me to a mixed school for my sins, and I did all right. What about you?" Kirkby said.

"It was Loreto for me. All girls, and some right bitches in amongst them too, I can tell you. But I stayed out of trouble, mostly. It's odd now meeting some of them as a Garda. I can't say I haven't had a bit of fun. Is that awful?"

Kirkby laughed.

"Dreadful! You wicked girl!"

"It's just here on the left. Would you like to come in, Vikki?"

"Ah, no, not this time. I'm a bit bushed to be honest, and I have loads to do at home. I'll see you tomorrow."

Kirkby pulled the car up on the side of a leafy lane.

Nestor smiled at her. "OK. Thanks for the lift." She opened the door and started to get out, then turned back. "And the answer is yes, and thanks for the opportunity."

"Great," Kirkby said. "See you tomorrow."

* * *

Kirkby drove back onto the main road, and on to the turn for Rosslare Strand. She wondered if she had done the right thing talking like that to Ciara Nestor. After her long stint in Dublin, she had forgotten just how parochial the country could be, and she hoped the young officer would respect her confidence and not make her life a misery when she got back in to work. Still, it would be a good test of Nestor's loyalty.

When she arrived at her temporary home, she noticed that nearly all the people who had been at the beach enjoying the warm June sunshine had departed, with just a few straggling couples dragging exhausted children along making their way back to their cars.

Kirkby went inside and prepared a crisp smoked salmon salad for herself, and opened a fresh bottle of chardonnay. She took her meal outside to the back garden, sat at the patio table, looking out over the broad, golden, sandy beach and marvelled at the beauty and peace of the place as the light breeze died down, as if it was going to sleep for the night, and the sun sank lower in the western sky.

Chapter Eight

As Kirkby arrived at the station the following morning, she met Jim Kennedy strolling across the car park towards the entrance.

"Good morning, Vikki. How are you settling in?"

"Hello, Jim. Yeah, things are going OK, thanks. Did you manage to have a word with Frawley about Ciara Nestor?"

"Yes, I did as it happens. Sorry, I should have called you. He's OK with it. He wasn't initially, but I told him to give you a break, and he agreed."

"Thanks, Jim. That'll be a big help to me. I really appreciate it," she said, putting her hand on his arm and squeezing it gently.

"No problem. Glad to help. How's the case going anyway?"

"We're just getting started, but it will be fine," she said, looking down at her shoes.

He held the door open for her, and once inside, they went their separate ways.

Kirkby was the first to arrive in the detectives' room. She went to her office, powered up her PC and started to go through the various emails and bulletins that arrived with monotonous regularity from Garda headquarters in Phoenix Park. After forty-five minutes, when it was just past nine o'clock, Cathal Waters arrived looking tired and somewhat dishevelled as usual.

"Good morning, boss," he said dropping down lazily into the seat in front of Kirkby's desk.

"Cathal, sit up for God's sake, and you really need to smarten up your dress. You look more like a hobo than a detective."

Waters shrugged and said nothing, so Kirkby continued, "Right, we have a lot on today. I want us to go out to the port and talk to Frank Roche's employers. I want to find out what he really did out there. Do you know if those boxes of paper were work-related?"

"I don't know, boss, I couldn't figure them out. But they'll be here later on today anyway. We can get someone to go over them."

"That someone could very easily be you, Cathal. Oh, and while I think of it, I'm co-opting Ciara Nestor to the team as a detective. We need more resources on this case."

Waters grunted.

"What?"

"Nothing, boss."

"No, tell me. If you have something on your mind, I want to hear it."

"Well, you could have consulted me. Have you spoken to Ciara?"

"Yes, she's fine with it, as is your friend, Superintendent Frawley."

Waters just sneered.

"OK, well, give me twenty minutes, then we'll head out to Rosslare. We'll go in my car. Could you ask Ciara to pop in for a minute please?"

Waters heaved himself up from his slouching position, and left rather grumpily without replying.

A few minutes later, Ciara Nestor knocked on Kirkby's door.

"Come in, Ciara. Take the weight off."

Nestor was still dressed in her Garda uniform. Kirkby was impressed that she had taken nothing for granted.

"Morning, boss. Everything OK?"

"Yes, sure. Look, that thing we were talking about last night, well it's been approved. I've told Sergeant Waters too, and he's fine with it," Kirkby said, stretching the truth a little.

"Cool. What do you want me to do then?" Nestor said.

"Today, I'd like you to make a start on the boxes of stuff that are coming in from the shed in the Roches' garden. Cathal doesn't know what it's all about, but there must be a reason why the man had all that paperwork stored at home. See if you can sort it in some way, and maybe run up a spreadsheet if you think it's appropriate. I'm sorry to lumber you with such a boring job, but someone has to do it."

"OK, well I'll get on with it then. Has the paperwork arrived in from Tobinstown?" Nestor said.

"Ask Cathal. He was looking after the transport. Oh, and Ciara, wear your own clothes from tomorrow, OK?"

"Yes, fine. Thanks, boss, and thanks again for the opportunity."

"Just make sure you don't let me down, Ciara."

"Don't worry, I won't."

* * *

It was a bright, sunny morning as they left Wexford heading for the Rosslare Europort ferry terminal. When Kirkby had been growing up, Rosslare Harbour was a sleepy place. There were just four services daily to and from South Wales, and then, just before Kirkby left the county to join the Gardaí, routes to France were established.

These days, it was a different matter. The port now had three full-sized ferry berths, and another, known as Fisherman's Quay, where smaller vessels such as coasters and fishing boats could tie up and unload. With more than thirty scheduled sailings a week to the UK, France and Spain, and with other occasional arrivals such as small cruise ships, the place was now extremely busy.

As they drove out along the N25, past Killinick and Tagoat, they met several large lorries coming the other way, some with French and even Polish registrations.

"There must be a ferry in just now, Cathal. Have you ever travelled on any of them from Rosslare?"

"I've been to England a few times. My mother has a sister who lives near Chippenham, and I've visited her."

"Ah, that's a nice part of England. Did you visit Bath or any of the other beauty spots near there?"

"Not really. We just stayed around her house mostly," Waters said.

Kirkby remained quiet for a few more kilometres, then said, "Have you had any further thoughts about the Roche case, Cathal?"

"I'm still thinking the most likely explanation is that it was self-inflicted. I mean, mister killed his wife, then managed somehow to do away with himself. I can't see any reason why anyone would want to eliminate those two."

"But the pathologist said that was impossible given the location of the gun," Kirkby said.

"Guns are funny things. If you're not holding a shotgun tightly when it discharges, it can fly around in any direction."

"Have we checked to see if Frank or Eileen had a shotgun license?" Kirkby asked.

"No. But I can do that later if you like."

"Yes, please. And while you're at it, I'd like you to check out both of their medical records. If what you say is correct, and it is somehow a murder-suicide, then maybe one or both of them were terminally ill."

As Kirkby drove into the harbour area, her mobile phone rang.

"DI Kirkby," she said, activating the Bluetooth arrangement in the car from a button on the steering wheel.

"Hello, Inspector. It's Aileen Brophy here. Have you got a second?"

"Oh, hello, Aileen. Yes, of course. What's up?"

"I've had a call from Bukowski in Waterford. He's done the post-mortems on your two victims, and he's come up with something a bit odd," the pathologist said.

"Oh. What's that?"

"He says he's almost certain that the man was killed first. Apparently, the gun that was used has a single trigger, and it fires the left barrel first. The shot from the left barrel emerges in a slightly different pattern from the shot from the right barrel, and he says it indicates that the male victim was shot with the left barrel, and then the woman got it with the right."

"I see. So that puts paid to any notion of a murder-suicide, then," Kirkby said, looking at her colleague.

"Yes. Well, I sort of knew that anyway, but yes, it confirms my suspicion. There's no way the woman could have shot her husband and then sat down in the chair and killed herself. It's just not feasible."

"OK, thanks, Aileen. Anything else?"

"Yes. There's a partial print on one of the cartridge cases. Forensics are working on it now. It's not much, but they might get enough to run it through the database. They'll know later on. Listen, could I ask you to liaise directly with Dr Bukowski now? I'm kinda busy up here, and I have another unexplained death to attend to in Sligo."

"Yes, of course. Thanks for your help," Kirkby said, pulling her car into one of the few available parking spaces outside the Europort offices.

Waters didn't say anything when Kirkby had finished the call, but she sensed that he wasn't too happy. They got out of the car and went inside.

Chapter Nine

The block occupied by the administrative offices of the harbour management company was a two-storey building that had been largely constructed of brown breeze blocks. It had a flat roof, and a lot of large aluminium windows, giving the occupants an excellent view of the entire area, and in particular the berths where the ferries docked. Inside the main door there was a reception area with pale-blue vinyl tiles on the floor and white walls. An office desk was positioned at an angle across the area, and behind it sat a woman in her late twenties, sporting a mid-blue suit with the Europort logo embroidered into the pocket of her jacket.

"Good morning. How can I help you?" she said, looking up from her PC.

Kirkby introduced them, and asked to see whoever was in charge.

"That's Mr Booth. His office is on the next floor." She indicated the utilitarian staircase with metal bannisters and a black handrail. "You can go on up. It's the last door on the left, and I'll let Mr Booth know you're coming."

They arrived at the door to the manager's office a few moments later, and Kirkby knocked.

"Come in," a voice invited from inside.

Kirkby opened the door and went into the spacious and well-appointed office, noting the commanding view that the room had out across the harbour. But when she saw who was occupying it, she got quite a surprise.

"Hello, Mr Booth. I'm Detective Inspector Vikki Kirkby, and this is my sergeant, Cathal Waters. But don't I know you?" she said.

"Well, well. Vikki Kirkby. Long time, no see," he said advancing towards her with his hand outstretched.

Booth was a slim man, of just over 180 cm tall. He was immaculately groomed, with neatly trimmed black hair, a handsome face, and he wore a navy suit, sparkling white shirt and silk tie along with highly polished black shoes.

"Gosh, Peter! I didn't expect to see you here. What must it be? More than twenty years, that's for sure."

Waters cleared his throat.

"Sorry, Cathal. Peter and I were at school together at Selskar. Well, he was a few years ahead of me of course, but we knew each other." And then turning back to Peter Booth, she said, "How have you ended up here, Peter?"

"After school I joined one of the ferry companies operating here as an able seaman. I worked my way up to captain, and when I'd been doing that for a few years, an opportunity came up in the office, so I took it. It was getting pretty boring just sailing between Rosslare and Wales twice a day, and the ships were becoming more and more automated, so the fun had gone out of it for me. But they still call me Captain Booth around here for some reason."

As if to make the point, there was a knock at the door, and a young man stuck his head around it.

"Sorry to disturb you, Captain, but the Cherbourg ferry wants to know if he can leave twenty minutes early. He's all loaded and closed up."

"Yes, Todd, that's cleared. Tell him to watch out for the lifeboat though. They're doing some training just outside the harbour. It wouldn't do if he ran over them. And be sure to enter the actual departure time in the log."

"Yes, of course. I'll ask him to call the lifeboat on the radio when he gets underway. Thanks." With that the young man disappeared.

"So, tell me about you, Vikki. I never saw you again after I left school. Where have you been hiding?" Booth said with a warm, open smile.

"Not much to tell. My dad wanted me to go into the bank, but I wasn't having it, so I ran away to join the Gardaí. I've been working in Dublin up to recently, but I've been posted to Wexford now, so here I am."

"Dublin's loss is Wexford's gain then. Anyway, what can I do for you today?"

Outside the window, the large, mostly white ferry, was preparing to get going. Thick black smoke poured from its funnel, and the water all around the ship was being churned up into a white froth from the propellors.

"It's about Frank Roche. I understand he worked here," Kirkby said.

"God, yes. An awful business. I'd no idea he was troubled to that extent. And his poor wife as well. Very tragic."

"What have you heard?" Kirkby said.

"News travel fast in the country, Vikki. I understand he shot his poor wife and then took his own life. Very sad."

Kirkby didn't bother to correct the man's impression.

"I suppose you have to look into these things though, even if it is clear-cut," Booth said.

"Yes, there are procedures to be followed."

Two large blasts on the departing ferry's horn interrupted their conversation for a few seconds as the ship gently moved sideways off the berth and then made for the gap between the two piers. Passengers could be seen on the decks enjoying the sunshine and waving to those left behind on dry land.

When peace was restored, Kirkby continued.

"What exactly did Frank Roche do here, Peter?"

"His official title was Loading Master. He was responsible for overseeing the loading and unloading of the ships. He also had to ensure that the vehicles coming off the ferries were compliant with their various certifications, and he was responsible for getting the dead trailers on and off too."

"Dead trailers?" Kirkby said.

"Yes. We carry a lot of trailer-only bookings. The haulage companies drop them off and allow the tractor units to leave and go and do more hauling. We have tugs that we connect up to the trailers and move them onto the ferry. Another similar operation takes place the far side. It's more economical for the haulage companies, and it takes up less room on the ship."

"I see. Is there much paperwork involved in Mr Roche's work?" Waters asked.

"Masses. We're trying to do more electronically, but this business is very paper-intensive still. It's very hard to move people off the old systems."

"And where is all that paper stored, Peter?"

"It's downstairs in a huge kind of warehouse at the back of the building. To be honest, we could burn the lot for all I care, but apparently it has to be kept for six years. Something to do with Customs and Excise."

"Can you think of anyone that might have wanted to harm Frank Roche?"

"No, of course not. But why is that an issue? It was suicide, wasn't it?"

"Yes, well, we better not keep you any longer, Peter. I'm sure you have plenty to do. Let me give you my contact details in case anything occurs to you when we've gone. And do you think we could have a quick look at the document store?"

Kirkby wrote her mobile phone number on a generic card from Wexford Regional Headquarters, as she hadn't yet received her personal business cards, and handed it to Peter Booth.

"Yes, of course. I'll get someone to show you down there. It's good to see you, Vikki. I hope it works out for you here."

"Thanks, Peter. We may be in touch again at some stage."

Captain Booth made a phone call, and a few moments later, Todd appeared again and escorted Kirkby and Waters downstairs and along a rather dim corridor to the storeroom. As Kirkby left his company, she remembered how and why he had been all the girls' heart-throb when they were at school. The butterflies in her stomach didn't seem to want to settle. Maybe this move back to Wexford holds some promise, after all, she thought to herself.

Downstairs, Todd opened the door to the storeroom, threw a switch, and an array of fluorescent lights that were suspended on chains from the ceiling flickered into life. The place had no windows.

All along the perimeter walls of the area, there were racks and racks of shelving, and nearly all of the shelves were laden with boxes, which Kirkby assumed were similar to the boxes that had been found in Frank Roche's shed. On one side of the facility, five grey, steel, four-drawer filing cabinets were positioned beside each other.

Kirkby strolled down along the leftmost aisle studying the shelving. The boxes were arranged by date and by ferry operator, and then by individual vessel. She selected a box marked 'Stena Europe, October 2020, Box 5'. She lifted the lid and peered inside. The box was full of pink and yellow NCR pages with various entries for different sailings. She lifted out a sheaf of the papers that were stapled together and turned to Todd who was still hovering nearby.

"Todd, any chance I could have a photocopy of this little bundle?" Kirkby said.

"Yes, I suppose so. Give it here and I'll be back in a minute."

Kirkby handed over the wad of paper, and Todd left the room.

"What's going on, boss?" Waters asked.

"Nothing. I just want to see if these match anything that was found in Roche's shed, that's all."

Waters just shrugged. Clearly, he was never going to understand her.

Todd returned a few minutes later with a large manilla envelope containing the copies, and he put the originals back in the box from which Kirkby had taken them.

"Thanks, Todd. That's it. We're ready to go now."

Chapter Ten

When Kirkby got back to the Garda station, she went in search of Ciara Nestor whom she found poring over documents that she had removed from some of the boxes that had been brought in from Frank Roche's shed.

"How's it going, Ciara?"

"Hello, boss. Slowly. But thankfully all the files are immaculately ordered, except for two boxes that were dropped by the transport people and got all muddled up," Nestor said, casting her eyes to heaven.

"Typical! Anyway, I have a few documents of my own that I fished out of a box labelled 'Stena Europe, October 2020, Box 5' out at the port. See if you can match them with anything from the shed, will you?" Kirkby said, handing over the envelope she had received from Todd.

"Oh, and there was a Danny Roche on the phone earlier. I think he's the son of the two deceased. He wants to come and see you. I said I'd get back to him to arrange a time."

"Thanks. Is he going to drive up from Cork?"

"Yes, I assume so. When would you like to see him?" Nestor said.

"Let's say 11 a.m. tomorrow. That will give him plenty of time to get here without having to leave at the crack of dawn. I think it's about a two-and-a-half-hour jaunt."

"Right. I'll call him in a few minutes and set it up. How did you get on?"

"Pretty good, really. I bumped into a guy I hadn't seen since we were at school together. Peter Booth by name, or should I say Captain Peter Booth. He's running the whole show out at the port now."

"Wow! That's a coincidence. Was he helpful?"

"Yes, but he wasn't able to throw any light on why the Roches should have met their end in such a gruesome way. Anyway, I'd better see what Sergeant Waters is up to. Catch you later."

* * *

Cathal Waters was at his desk tucking into a rather messy cream doughnut and a cup of coffee when Kirkby approached. She looked disapprovingly at the state of his desk, covered in icing sugar and discarded wrappers as it was. Waters picked up on her unspoken message.

"It's lunchtime boss," he said, wiping his mouth with the back of his hand.

"Yes, so I see. Have we anything more back on Frank Roche yet?"

"Yes. I was just about to come and find you. Firstly, neither of them had a shotgun license, and I don't think they had a shotgun either. The neighbour told me he never knew Roche to be involved in shooting. They weren't the type, it seems."

"So that means that the gun was left behind by the killer or killers. Have we been able to do anything with the serial number?" Kirkby asked.

"Eh… no. I haven't got that far yet. I'll give Keith in forensics a call when I get a chance. But I have the Roches' bank account details coming in later on this afternoon. The bank was quite awkward about it, but when I threatened the manager with a warrant and several uniformed Gardaí arriving at his branch with blue lights and sirens, he soon changed his tune," Waters said, smirking.

"Good, well done. Maybe that will tell us something. I'll be in my office if you need me."

* * *

Back in the relative calm of her own much-improved office, with the door closed, Kirkby had time to organise her thoughts. She was aware that she was being closely observed by virtually everyone at the station, and Frawley in particular. She couldn't afford to slip up on this case, but the trouble was, she didn't seem to be getting anywhere. Here was a perfectly ordinary bloke and his wife, or so it seemed from what they knew so far, and they had been cut down in what was by any measure a fairly brutal manner by persons unknown. And for what? She knew that she needed to produce something significant very soon, or without doubt, the case would be taken away from her, and she would be once again scapegoated as being the cause of the failure. Vikki Kirkby was not about to allow that to happen.

She was still pondering her fate when her desk phone burst into life, disturbing her thoughts.

"DI Kirkby."

"Hello, Inspector. This is Keith Sexton from forensics. I'm calling about the gun that was recovered from the scene out at Tobinstown."

"Hi, Keith. What have you got?"

"Quite a bit. Firstly, it looks as if the gun is Spanish. There has been some attempt to obliterate the numbers with acid, but we were still able to reveal them. The markings on the stock are 57-03-9177-09. That tells us, if we are correct, that it was manufactured in 2009 by a company called Arrieta – that's the 57 element. The 03 just defines it as a shotgun, and the 9177 is the maker's serial number. Arrieta make very high-class guns. They're located in the north of Spain and have a great reputation. This one would have been very expensive when it was sold originally," Sexton said.

"Have you any idea if these guns are sold in Ireland?"

"No, sorry, but I doubt it. It seems, looking at their website, that most of their production is bespoke. A bit like Purdey in the UK."

"What does that mean, Keith?"

"It means each gun is made for a specific user. The stock is fashioned to fit the reach and shoulder of the owner to minimise recoil and ensure that it is comfortable to use. It would have cost a few thousand when new, and it's in good condition."

"I see. Anything else?"

"No, sorry, not for now at least. We're still working on the partial from the cartridge, but I'm not too hopeful on that score."

"Any idea where the cartridges came from?"

"Yes. They're Spanish too. Made by Eurotrap. It's apparently a fairly common brand."

"OK. Well, can you send me all that by email, and let me know if you get anything else useful. Thanks."

"Sure. It's on its way."

"Cheers, Keith."

A few moments later, Kirkby's email program pinged on her PC as the report from Keith Sexton arrived in her inbox. When she had opened it, and read the contents, she looked up the Arrieta website and found contact details for the company. She dialled the phone number displayed at the foot of the web page.

"*Buenas tardes, dígame*," said the voice of a Spanish woman at the other end of the line.

Kirkby had a small smattering of Spanish from a few holidays that she had taken in the country over the years, but she was by no means fluent.

"*Habla Inglés?*" Kirkby said hopefully.

"*Lo siento, no. Momentito,*" the woman said, and the call went to music as Kirkby was put on hold.

A few moments later, a female voice, speaking English with just a hint of an accent, came on the line.

"Good afternoon. My name is Margarita Lopez. Who am I speaking to?"

"Good afternoon, Ms Lopez. This is Detective Inspector Vikki Kirkby from the Irish police. I wonder if you can help me?"

"Oh, hello. I hope so, officer. What is it that you require?"

"I'm investigating an incident here in the south-east of Ireland, and we have recovered a shotgun from the scene. We believe it may have been manufactured by your company."

"I see. Do you have a serial number?" Lopez said.

"Yes, I have it here. Just a moment." She quickly switched her PC from Arrieta's website into her email application where Keith's report was still open. "It's 57-03-9177-09."

"Yes, well that looks like one of ours all right, although it's quite old now. But our shotguns are built to last. What can I help you with?"

"I know this may be tricky, but I was hoping you might be able to tell me who the gun was sold to, or perhaps the person you made it for."

"We will have records, for sure. But it will take me some time to locate that information. And perhaps your enquiry needs to come through the Guardia Civil. I'll have to check that too. There is data protection to consider."

"I see. It would be very helpful if we could deal directly with one another, Ms Lopez. It was a very serious incident, and we need to keep the delays to a minimum if we are to have any chance of catching the perpetrator."

"I'll see what I can do, Inspector. May I have your direct phone number?"

Kirkby reeled off her mobile number, remembering to put the 00 353 in front of it, and thanked the woman for her help.

"I'll try and get back to you tomorrow, Inspector. Is that OK?"

"Yes, of course. Thanks again. Bye."

Chapter Eleven

Late in the afternoon, Kirkby gathered the team around her in the detectives' open-plan office for a briefing.

"Right, everyone. I have some new information concerning the gun that was used to kill the Roches, but first I want to hear what you have got from the day's work. Cathal, let's start with you."

Waters shifted a little uneasily in his chair.

"I got the Roches' bank statements a little while ago from the bank in town. I had a quick look. There doesn't seem to be anything odd in them. I can see his salary from the harbour company coming in each month, and then all the usual stuff going out – you know, property tax, electricity bill, various payments for what look like groceries and so on. Nothing untoward, boss."

"Except that we know they had a separate Credit Union account with a pretty hefty balance," Kirkby said.

"Yes, of course, I'd forgotten about that," Waters said.

"What have you got for us, Ciara?"

"I've been going through all that paperwork, boss. I found copies of the paperwork from the port in one of the boxes and it seems like Frank had put an asterisk beside an entry where the trailer number was listed, and highlighted it in yellow marker. There are other pages where he has done the same thing too, but I have no idea why. They just look like ordinary movements to me, but I'm not an expert."

"Interesting. Could you take a sample of, say, fifty sets of documents from different boxes and create a spreadsheet with all the details of the lines that have an asterisk beside them? We might be able to find a trend in the data somehow."

"Yes, OK, boss. Oh, and by the way, Danny Roche will be here in the morning at eleven to see you."

"Good, thanks, Ciara. Well, let's leave it at that for now then."

"Sorry, boss, but did you say you had more information about the gun?" Nestor said.

"Oh, yes, sorry. Thanks for reminding me," Kirkby said. She went on to relay the information about the shotgun and the conversation with the Spanish company. When she had finished, she said to Waters, "Cathal, a word in my office please."

Waters looked uneasy as he followed her into her office and closed the door.

"Look, Cathal, I've mentioned this before, and I'm not delighted at having to bring it up again. You need to smarten yourself up. Get a new outfit that doesn't look as if you've slept in it. And no more eating messy cakes at your desk. If you need a snack or lunch, go to the canteen. I'm not having one of my team looking like they've just raided the school tuckshop. Do I make myself clear?"

"Yes, boss."

"And another thing. Keith from forensics got to me before you had called him, as I asked you to do. You need to sharpen your act up big time, Cathal, or we're going to have a serious falling-out. Do you understand?"

Waters was looking down at the carpet.

"Well? And look at me when I'm speaking to you!" Kirkby added, raising her voice a little.

"Yes, boss. But can I say something?" Waters said.

"No, you can't. Next time I see you, I want to be looking at someone who looks like a detective. Now if you hurry, you'll just be in time to catch a decent clothes shop in town. We're done."

* * *

At six o'clock, Kirkby collected her stuff and left the station. She wasn't her usual happy self. Progress was much too slow for her liking, and she was becoming frustrated. She also wasn't looking forward to having to reprimand her detective sergeant further if he didn't shape up. But when she got out on the N25, heading for Rosslare, her humour improved. The sun was still shining, and somehow, as she drove along, the view out across the well-tended fields lifted her spirits, and her troubles seemed to fall away.

At home, once she had changed out of her work clothes, Kirkby opened a bottle of white wine that she had cooling in the fridge, and set about preparing a chicken salad. She was in the middle of the task when much to her surprise the doorbell rang. When she opened the door, Peter Booth was standing on the step with a big broad grin on his face.

"Oh, hello, Peter," she said a little flustered by his presence, "what brings you here?"

"I was just on my way home, and I thought I'd drop in to see how you were getting on?"

"Right. Well, you'd better come in," she said standing back to allow him to enter the house.

When they got to the kitchen, she said, "How did you know where to find me?"

"Small town, Vikki. Anyway, your landlord is an acquaintance of mine from the rugby club, and he was telling us about his good fortune in getting a long tenancy from a pretty detective Garda recently. So, two plus two, etc."

"Maybe it's you that should be the detective! Sorry, would you like a glass of wine? It's only white I'm afraid. And I might be able to stretch this chicken salad to two portions if you're not too hungry?"

"I have a better idea. Why don't we go out to eat? We could nip over to the Lobster Pot in Carne. They're open till nine."

"Eh… well, I suppose we could. Won't there be anyone at home expecting you though?"

"No," Booth said. "I'm not married or anything. I was, but we split up three years ago, and I've been a bachelor again ever since."

"Sorry, I didn't mean to pry," Kirkby said, her cheeks reddening slightly.

"Ah, don't worry. What about you? Is there a Mr Vikki?"

"Absolutely not! And no Mrs Vikki either, before you ask," she said smiling. "Just give me a few minutes to get ready and I'll be with you then."

Kirkby appeared back in the kitchen ten minutes later looking radiant in a pale summer dress, and with her hair nicely combed out and hanging loosely over her shoulders.

Booth beamed at her. "Wow! You look great, Vikki. Ready?"

"Yes. Let's go!"

* * *

The Lobster Pot is a low-rise building that occupies a fork in the road on the way down to Carne Beach. It is renowned for its seafood dishes, and the proprietors oversee the running of the place every night, ensuring a very high standard is maintained. They had travelled out in Peter Booth's Skoda Superb, which Kirkby found very comfortable and spacious. Booth had been a proper gentleman, opening the door for her when they got into the car, and again when they arrived.

"I hope you're hungry," he said as they strolled across the car park to the narrow entrance.

"Starving! You?"

"I'll manage," he said, with that cheeky grin that Kirkby was beginning to get used to.

Once seated, they ordered their food and drinks.

"I'll stick to water," Booth said, "I wouldn't want you to have to arrest me for drink-driving, Inspector!"

"And don't think I wouldn't, Captain Booth," she replied, smiling.

As the evening wore on, Booth tried subtly to probe the matter of the Roches' death, but Kirkby was having none of it.

"I'm sorry, Peter, I can't discuss any aspect of the case with you," she said, "after all, you may have information that is relevant as a witness, so let's just leave it, OK?"

"Yes. Of course, sorry. I didn't realise it was so sensitive."

Once that topic was off the table, they chatted easily about the old days in Wexford, and how some of the other pupils at the school that they both knew had fared. Booth was still in touch with some of them, and Kirkby remembered one or two of the names he came up with. The time slipped by till the restaurant was starting to close up.

"We'd better get out of here, Peter. I think they're closing."

"Oh, yes, you're right," he said, observing the clattering of cutlery and the cleaning of the tables that the waiting staff were enthusiastically engaged in.

They left the premises and drove back to Rosslare Strand. Before any awkwardness could arise, Kirkby made the position clear to her impromptu date.

"I'm not going to invite you in, Peter. I have a tough day tomorrow, and in any case, it might give some people the wrong impression. But thank you for the meal, it was lovely." She leaned across and giving him a perfunctory peck on the cheek. She quickly opened the car door and climbed out.

As she walked up the short path to her front door, Booth called out the window of his car, "Maybe we can do it again sometime?"

"Yes, maybe. Goodnight." She turned and went indoors.

Once inside the house, she checked to see that Booth had driven off before she relaxed fully. She wondered if she had been too stand-offish with him. He was a very good-looking man after all, and she could do with some male company, but was it a good idea?

"This could get complicated," she said to herself as she ascended the stairs.

Chapter Twelve

As soon as Kirkby got to the station the following morning, she called Ciara Nestor and Cathal Waters into her office. She noted that Waters still looked very scruffy. She was disappointed that he had not addressed the issue.

"OK, folks, what have we got that we didn't have yesterday?"

Waters said nothing, so after a short and somewhat embarrassing silence, Ciara Nestor spoke up.

"I've been doing a bit of analysis on the documents you gave me, boss. You know, the entries that Mr Roche had put the asterisk alongside. Well, the cargo in each of those cases is Spanish, but it came in on UK trucks. I haven't been able to figure out exactly what was going on yet."

"Maybe the cargo went by ship from Spain to the UK somewhere and then was offloaded into the trucks and brought across. What sort of stuff was in the loads, Ciara?" Kirkby said.

"All sorts. Quite a lot of fruit, mostly oranges, lemons and some tomatoes, but other stuff too like furniture, household appliances and textiles."

"That seems pretty detailed. Did you get all that information from the paperwork?"

"Yes. Since Brexit, there's a lot more detail on goods entering Ireland from the UK."

"Oh, right, yes of course," Kirkby said, although she hadn't any experience in this area herself.

"So! Spanish goods that seem to have been of interest to Roche, and a Spanish gun that killed him. Coincidence?" Kirkby said, looking at Waters.

"Could be, I guess, but maybe not," Waters said with little enthusiasm.

"OK. Well, we have Danny Roche coming in at eleven, so can you keep going with your analysis of the paperwork, Ciara? Cathal and I will talk to the son. If anything else odd pops up, be sure to let me know."

"Right, boss."

* * *

Danny Roche arrived at the Garda station at 10:50. The desk sergeant called Kirkby on the internal phone and told her of his arrival.

"I'll be down in a few minutes to collect him, Sarge."

She then went and alerted Cathal Waters and asked him to accompany her downstairs to conduct an interview with the young man.

Danny Roche was a tall, thin man in his late twenties with a mop of curly blonde hair and a thin, oval face. He was dressed casually in smart khaki-coloured slacks and a navy pullover and good black leather shoes.

"Good morning, Mr Roche. My name is Detective Inspector Vikki Kirkby, and this is my sergeant, Cathal Waters. Thanks for coming in to see us, and I'm very sorry for your loss. It must be dreadful to lose both parents in such tragic circumstances."

"Thanks, Inspector. I'm hoping you'll be able to help me understand what happened."

"Let's go in here and we can have a chat. Can I get you a cup of tea or coffee? You must be parched after that drive," Kirkby said, indicating a door with 'Family Room' displayed on it.

"Thanks. A coffee would be great. Milk, no sugar."

Kirkby nodded to Waters, who said, "Would you like one too, Inspector?"

"No thanks, Cathal. I'm fine."

Waters shuffled off to see to the visitor's drink, while Kirkby and Roche sat opposite each other across the melamine-covered table. Danny Roche was the first to speak.

"Have you found out what happened to my parents, Inspector?" Roche said.

"It's very early days still, Mr Roche. We're just starting to collect evidence. Obviously, we know that your parents were killed deliberately, but as to motive, or who may have been responsible, I'm afraid we haven't made a lot of progress. But as I said it's early days. Do you mind if I ask you some questions?"

"No, of course not. I'm here to help, if I can," the young man said.

"When did you last see your parents, Mr Roche?"

"Please, call me Danny. Everyone does. Two weeks ago. I try to visit every two weeks if I can, work permitting of course."

"And what exactly do you do in Cork?"

"I'm a customs officer. I'm involved in the inspection of goods coming into the country on the ferries and ro-ro vessels, and the associated paperwork. It's mostly fairly straightforward. We get a bit of smuggling of course, but nothing too serious. It's mostly concealed narcotics these days. You know, cannabis and cocaine hidden in amongst the cargo."

Waters came into the room with Danny Roche's coffee, and one for himself. He had managed to find a few chocolate biscuits to go with the drink.

"Thanks, Cathal. Danny was telling me about his work in Cork as a customs officer," Kirkby said.

"Oh, right," Waters said, joining his boss at the table.

"Did you ever talk to your father about his work out at Rosslare, Danny?" Kirkby said.

"A bit, I suppose. It's only natural as we're both in similar occupations, albeit he worked for Europort, not Customs," Danny said.

"What sort of things did he tell you about the comings and goings in Rosslare?" Kirkby said.

"Nothing very specific. We just chatted about some of the ships and the new services that are being introduced. That sort of thing."

"Did he say anything about British lorries coming in with Spanish cargos?" Kirkby said.

"No. Why? Is that relevant to what happened?"

"We don't know yet. Did you know, Danny, that your father had boxes and boxes of copied paperwork stored in that secure shed in the back garden of your parents' house?"

"No. No, I didn't. What sort of paperwork?"

"We're still looking into it, but it appears to be copies of bills of lading and information about cargoes and vessel movements at the port. He seems to have had some interest in loads coming from Spain via the UK. Does that mean anything to you?" Kirkby said.

Danny shook his head from side to side, with a puzzled look on his face.

"No. I'm afraid not. I had no idea he was doing that at all. He never said."

"How long had he had the shed?" Waters said.

"It appeared about four or five years ago, Sergeant. They had quite a job getting the sections in through the back gate. I think they had to crane some of the bigger ones over the wall," Roche said.

"What did he tell you he wanted it for?" Kirkby said.

"He didn't. I just assumed it was for tools or something. But now that you mention it, it was very big for a few garden implements."

"And you honestly never discussed the shed or its contents?"

"No. Never. But listen, have you no idea who was responsible for this horrible crime? Someone must have heard something or seen something. It's quite a remote area. Any strangers kicking around would have been very obvious."

"I know, Danny. It's quite a mystery. But don't worry, we won't stop until we have solved this case and brought the perpetrators to book. We can't have this kind of thing going on and people getting away with it. Can I ask you, Danny, did your father ever own a shotgun?"

"No, of course not. Is that how they were killed?"

"Yes, I'm afraid so. But it would have been quick, at least. They wouldn't have known much about it. Tell me, Danny, did your parents have any connection with Spain at all?" Kirkby said.

"I don't think so. We went there a few times on holiday when I was growing up. But I don't think there was any other connection. Why?"

"Oh, it's probably nothing. What about you? Do you have any Spanish connections?"

"No. None at all. You must have a reason for asking, Inspector?"

Kirkby gave Waters a sharp look. She didn't want him to give anything away.

"No, as I said, it's probably nothing. So, have you any other information that you think might help us to uncover a motive for your parents' murder, Danny? Who did they socialize with, for example?"

"I'm not sure, Inspector. I don't think they had much of a social life. They were both pretty busy with work. But my mam used to visit her sister in England once a year during the school holidays."

"Did your father go with her?" Waters asked.

"Not every year, but sometimes, yes."

"Well, Danny, if there's nothing else, then I'm not sure if we can help you any further at this stage. But I'd like to thank you for driving up to see us, and I'll keep in touch as things develop. Before you go, would you mind if we took your fingerprints and a DNA sample? We need to eliminate your prints from the house, for obvious reasons," Kirkby said.

"That's no problem. Obviously, I'm keen to help in any way I can. And it's good to meet the people at the leading edge of the investigation. May I keep in touch with you both?"

"Yes, of course," Kirkby said, scribbling her mobile number on a generic business card and handing it to the young man.

Waters took Danny Roche out to have his fingerprints recorded and get a DNA swab. After he'd seen the young man off the premises, he made his way back to Kirkby's office where she was mulling over the interview.

"What do you think, boss?"

"I'm not sure. He didn't seem as upset as I thought he would be. And it's more about what he didn't say, than what he did. That was a good question you asked him about the shed, by the way."

Waters smiled slightly. He was pleased to receive praise from his boss after her previous comments about him.

"Yeah, I think it's very odd that he didn't know a bit more about it. And I think that shed and its content may well be the key to this whole thing," Waters said.

"You could be right, Cathal. Did you manage to clock what kind of car he was driving?"

"Yes. Rather a nice black BMW on last year's plate. I took a note of the number too, just for the record," Waters said.

"Good. Well done. Now, can you get those prints over to Keith in forensics so he can match them to any he found at the scene."

"Yes sure, boss. See you later."

Chapter Thirteen

Following the interview with Danny Roche, Kirkby wanted to go back out to the port to have another word with Peter Booth. She felt that it would be no harm to see him again in any case. He might even be prompted to ask her out, if she played her cards right. Before she left with her sergeant in tow, she went to the bathroom to make sure that her hair was nicely brushed and her makeup was the best she could get it.

"C'mon, Cathal. Let's get out to Rosslare. I want to have another chat with Mr Booth."

Waters wasn't sure what exactly was happening, but he fell in behind his boss willingly enough.

"Yours or mine, boss?" he said, referring to the cars.

"What's yours like? Have you cleaned it up at all?"

Waters said nothing, but blipped the key fob in his hand to open the doors. Kirkby went over to the sergeant's car, and opened the front passenger door, not quite knowing what to expect. As soon as she opened the door a fresh smell of polish greeted her, and the next thing she noticed was that the car was immaculate inside. The seats were clean, the carpets in the footwell looked new, with not a crumb or fragment of potato crisp in sight, and the dashboard was gleaming. She sat in, smiling to herself.

"What do you think?" Waters said as he slid in behind the steering wheel.

"Very nice. I don't feel as if I'm going to catch anything from it anymore. Did you do it yourself?"

"No. It was too scruffy for that. I took it into town to a car valeting place. They do a really nice job, and now that it's all nice and clean, it will be easy to keep it that way."

"Yes, it should be. But it's a much nicer place to be. Thanks."

Waters started the car and drove out of the station car park towards Rosslare. It was a nice sunny summer day as they drove out along the N25. There were a few cotton-wool clouds high up in the sky, but there would be no rain. The beaches of Carne, Rosslare and the other smaller ones in the area would be thronged with people enjoying the holiday atmosphere and the good weather.

The two detectives pulled up in front of the Europort office building and got out. Once inside, the same receptionist called upstairs to the main office, and they were asked to go on up.

Booth opened the door of his office to greet them as they approached.

"Good morning, Inspector, Sergeant. To what do I owe the pleasure of your company today?" he said with a broad, welcoming smile.

"We just wanted to clarify a few things with you, Mr Booth," Kirkby said.

"Please, it's Peter. And can I offer you a tea or a coffee?"

Kirkby sensed Waters was about to accept, so she said quickly, "No, we're fine thanks. We won't keep you long."

"Well, come in. Take a seat," he said gesturing to the two chairs in front of his desk.

As they walked across the room to sit down, Kirkby looked out across the harbour to the sea where the deep blue of the St George's Channel was glistening in the sunlight.

"Now, what's on your mind?" Booth said.

"We've done analysis on some paperwork that Frank Roche had secured at his home. It looks as if he had a special interest in trucks that were coming into the country carrying goods from Spain. They appear to be British wagons, but the contents were Spanish. Have you any idea why that might be, Mr Booth?"

Booth put his hand to his chin, and moved his head slowly from side to side.

"No, I haven't. Quite a bit of the freight through here comes across the land-bridge from the Continent. It's a bit trickier since Brexit, but all the customs stuff is handled electronically, so the lorries aren't delayed too much."

"And why would the goods not be in Spanish trucks?" Waters asked.

"A lot of it is. But some of it comes by sea from Spain to the ports in the south of England and is then transferred to articulated vehicles to travel on here. Apparently, it's cheaper than sending the goods by road all up through France and so on."

"I see. We noticed that Frank Roche seems to have a special interest in lorries from Tiverton Transport. Does that name ring a bell with you at all?" Kirkby asked.

"Not especially. I think I've seen their trucks rolling off the ferry. Big white refrigerated jobs with a blue-and-white tractor unit. The name of the company is plastered across the front above the windscreen," Booth said.

"And do they get inspected by Customs?" Kirkby asked.

"Occasionally. But, as I said, the processing is moving to electronic nowadays, so they usually just check in with Customs, get their clearance form and leave pretty soon after they disembark. The clearance cert is checked at the exit from the port. But Customs do sometimes look inside the containers to make sure that whatever has been declared is actually what is being carried. But they don't like to hold the drivers up. They often have to drive to Dublin, and want to get on with it."

"I see. So, in theory, there could be anything in those wagons?" Waters said.

"You have a suspicious mind, Sergeant. I'm not saying there isn't the odd bottle of cheap brandy that slips through, or maybe a few cigarettes, but the customs lads know what they're about. There's no major smuggling going on here."

"Yes, but Frank Roche must have been interested for a reason, don't you think? He went to a lot of trouble to keep records," Waters said.

"I don't know what he was up to, Sergeant. Now, if there's nothing else, we have a ferry due in shortly and I need to oversee the berthing and so on," Booth, standing up.

"OK, no worries. Thanks for seeing us in any case. We'll be in touch," Kirkby said, getting up and heading for the door.

Waters left the room first, and as he disappeared down along the corridor towards the stairs, Booth said quietly, "Vikki, just a sec."

Kirkby stopped and turned towards the man.

"I was wondering if you'd be free some evening for dinner," he said. "Maybe tonight?"

"Oh, yes, thanks, that would be lovely," she replied, checking to ensure that her sergeant was out of earshot.

"Great. I'll pick you up around 7:30 then, OK?"

"Yes, fine. Looking forward to it," she said, smiling.

When she rejoined her partner out in the car park, she was still smirking slightly.

"Everything OK, boss?" Waters said.

"Yes, perfectly fine thanks, Cathal, perfectly fine."

As she got into the car, she looked up at Booth's office window to see him looking down at them. He gave a little wave and was smiling broadly as she closed the car door.

As they drove back towards Wexford, Waters said, "What did you make of all that then?"

"Hmm… I think there's something going on that we need to explore further. Seems to me that there may be a fairly serious smuggling racket going on here. What do you think?"

"It looks a bit like that, all right. What are you going to do, boss?"

"I'm not sure just yet. But there's obviously something dodgy about those Tiverton Transport lorries. Let me think about it a little."

They completed the remainder of the journey in silence.

Chapter Fourteen

Back at the station, Kirkby was having trouble getting Peter Booth out of her head. She was definitely attracted to him, she thought, or was it just that there had been a drought in her love life for a good long time now, and she was getting desperate! No, she mused. He had always been every girl's dream when they were at school, and his attraction hadn't faded. Not as far as she was concerned anyway.

She was lost in her thoughts when she was interrupted by the phone ringing.

"Kirkby," she said, refocusing on the job in hand.

"Hello, Inspector. It's Keith here from forensics. Sorry it's taken me a while to get back to you, but we had to dig a little deeper on this one than usual."

"What one is that, Keith?"

"Sorry, the partial print that we recovered from the shooting out at Tobinstown. Remember?"

"Yes, of course, Keith. What have you got?"

"We think the print belongs to one Francisco Hernandez, a bad boy that has quite a sheet with the Spanish police. We had nothing that matched here, so we went to Europol and they found a match."

"I see. What degree of certainty, Keith? After all, it was only a partial print."

"From the actual print, about seventy percent. But from what the Guardia Civil told us, I'd say more like ninety percent. Hernandez has a history of violent crime. He's done three years in Spain for aggravated robbery, and there's a warrant out for him on an ABH as well," Sexton said.

"Christ! That's all we need. A bloody dangerous Spaniard running amok in County Wexford. Well, thanks anyway, Keith. That's a good bit of detecting on your part. Have we got a mug shot of this Hernandez bloke?"

"I asked the cops in Madrid to send one over. I'll forward it to you when I get it."

"OK, thanks."

When the call was over, Kirkby called Ciara Nestor into her office.

"Hi, Ciara. I've got something a bit more interesting for you." Kirkby told Nestor about the call from Keith.

"When the mug shot arrives, I want you to circulate it to the guest houses and hotels in the Rosslare area. I'd say this guy would probably stay somewhere cheap, so the B & Bs will likely be more productive. He may also have used a false name, so get them to go by the photograph. OK?"

"Cripes, boss, there are a hell of a lot of them to cover. The place is littered with B & Bs out there. And what if he stayed in an Airbnb? We'll never find him."

"Let's just hope we get lucky, Ciara. Remember this job is ten percent inspiration and ninety percent perspiration. Can you liaise with Keith about the mug shot?"

"Yes, of course. Wish me luck!"

"Good luck. And ask Cathal to pop in, will you?"

"Yes, sure," Nestor said, getting up and leaving the room.

A few moments later, Waters knocked on Kirkby's door and came into the office.

"You were looking for me, boss."

"Yes, come in. Sit down. I've been thinking, Cathal. We need to arrange a joint operation with Customs and Excise out at the port. I think there must be drugs or something in those Tiverton Transport lorries, and I want to put an end to it, and hopefully expose the Roches' killers at the same time."

"Wow! That's a bit of a tall order, boss. Are you sure?"

"Yes, I am. And I don't want Frawley to know about it till it's done and dusted, is that clear?" Kirkby said.

"Yes, but how are you going to organise it without him signing off on it?" Waters said.

"You leave that to me. Just be ready when I give the word. We'll need to get as many uniformed officers as we can, and all of us, of course, and we'll need to line up Customs and Excise too. Do you know anyone from Customs out at the port?"

"No, I'm afraid not, boss."

"Never mind. I'll sort that out too."

"When are you planning this operation, boss?"

"Sometime over the next few days. I'll let you know when I have it organised."

"OK. Is that all for now?"

"Yes, off you go. And remember, mum's the word."

When Cathal Waters had left the office, Kirkby got up from her desk and closed the door. She then looked up the number for Europort and dialled. The phone was answered promptly, presumably by the young woman that manned the reception desk at their offices.

"May I speak to Peter Booth, please?" Kirkby said.

"Hold on please, I'll see if he's available. Who shall I say is calling?"

"Inspector Kirkby from the Gardaí."

"Just a moment."

After the briefest spell of music, Booth came on the line.

"Hi, Vikki. I hope you're not calling to cancel our date," he said.

"Hi, Peter. No, of course not. I'm looking for a contact in the Customs and Excise out there though. Who's in charge?"

"That would be Gerry Healy. Why?"

"I need to speak to him. Have you a number for him?"

"Yes, of course. Hold on."

Booth was back on the line a few moments later and reeled off a phone number which Kirkby took down.

"Can I ask what you want him for?"

"No, you can't. But thanks for the contact anyway. See you later."

"Yes, 7:30. Bye."

The next call she made was to Inspector Jim Kennedy. She explained what she had in mind, and asked if he could arrange a warrant to enable her plan to go ahead.

"I can, but wouldn't you be better asking Frawley?"

"I don't want to do that for various reasons, Jim. And I'd be obliged if you wouldn't say anything to him about it either. He'll hear about it soon enough."

"OK, then. Pop up in half an hour or so, and I'll have it signed off here for you."

Kirkby knew she was going out on a limb, but she couldn't afford to be stopped from executing her plan by Frawley. That would mean total loss of face, and she doubted if she would ever recover her reputation that way. Anyway, she reassured herself, her instincts were good, and the circumstantial evidence was strong, so she wasn't too bothered about it all going pear-shaped.

Chapter Fifteen

Peter Booth arrived at Kirkby's rented house in Rosslare Strand at exactly 7:30. The inspector had taken some trouble over her appearance. She had showered and washed her hair as soon as she got in from the office, and had selected a lightweight summer outfit and open-toed sandals to wear, with a light woollen cardigan, in case it got a bit cooler later on. A gleaming gold necklace with a heart-shaped locket set off her outfit and matched the gold wristwatch that she had been given by her parents when she turned eighteen. Kirkby checked herself in the mirror in the hall, and was pleased with the overall effect.

When she opened the door, Booth was standing there clutching a bunch of gorgeous flowers that had quite obviously come from an expensive florist, and not from a petrol station. She observed that he too had taken trouble with his outfit. He wore pale-coloured chinos, a well-ironed button-down check shirt and a linen jacket, as well as highly polished black leather shoes.

"Aw, thanks, Peter. They're beautiful. You're very kind," she said accepting the flowers. "Come in. I'll put these in water. Can I get you a coffee or anything?"

"No thanks, Vikki. We'd better be going anyway. I have a table booked for eight in town."

"Oohh nice. Where are you taking me?"

"It's a surprise! You're looking lovely this evening, by the way." He leaned into her and gave her a light kiss on the cheek.

They went outside, and Kirkby locked the door carefully behind them. Booth's car was at the side of the road gleaming in the evening sunlight, and he opened the passenger's door for her.

"How do you keep your car so clean, Peter? It's always spotless. And the roads are very dusty at this time of year."

"Ah, well, you see, there's a vehicle wash down at the port. It was left over after the foot-and-mouth thing a few years back, and it's excellent. Very thorough. I just run it through that every few days, but don't tell anyone."

Kirkby laughed.

"Don't worry. Your secret is safe with me!"

"Tell me, Vikki, are you OK with seafood again?" Booth said.

"Oh, yes, please. I love it."

"Good, cos that's where we're going. Wexford's finest!"

"Great. I hope they do a nice chilled white wine too!"

"You can bank on it."

* * *

When they were seated at a table overlooking the harbour on the first floor of Bia na Mara, which translated from Irish means 'food from the sea', Booth broached the subject of the current investigation.

"So, how's the Roche case going for you, Vikki?"

"I can't really say anything about it, Peter, as it's an ongoing investigation. But I think we're making some progress."

"Can I ask why you wanted Gerry Healy's phone number?"

Kirkby could see that he wasn't going to give up, so she decided she had better tell him something.

"Look, Peter, I have to be very careful what I say. If word got out it could blow a big operation. But we are going to have a good close look at some of the vehicles that come off one of the ferries. And that's all I'm saying. Sorry."

"I understand. Say no more. How did you end up back here anyway?" Booth asked. "Did you decide it was time to come home?"

"No, not a bit of it. I was the number two on a really big organised crime case in Dublin. To make a long story short, the SIO, another DI – male of course – made a mess of the evidence. He failed to inform the defence about some CCTV material we were relying on to put a nasty bit of stuff away for a nice long time. The case fell apart, and the judge gave us a good bollocking. Basically, although it wasn't my fault, I was scapegoated and offered the choice of a downgrade in rank or a posting to the sticks."

"I see. Well, we don't think of Wexford as the sticks as you call it."

"No, I know, and I didn't mean to be insulting. After all, this is my hometown too. But you know what I mean. And now of course, my superintendent here is just waiting for me to slip up so he can agree with his buddies in Dublin that I'm a waste of space."

"Charming! Do you think it's because you're a woman?" Booth said.

"It's probably got a good bit to do with it. Despite a lot of soundbites in the media, An Garda Síochána is still quite male-dominated, especially amongst the senior, and hence older, officers."

"But didn't you have a female commissioner for a while?"

"Yes, we did. And as you may recall, that didn't end well either."

"More misogyny?"

"Who knows. Some say she wasn't much good. That she was just put in there as a token female, but I don't know. I never met the woman. I wouldn't like to judge."

"So, will you be OK on this caper?"

"I bloody hope so. Otherwise, it's traffic duty in north Donegal for me!"

The rest of the meal was passed with more chit-chat about the past, and what Booth had been doing since they left school. The food was delicious, and Kirkby managed two quite substantial glasses of chardonnay, while Booth stuck to alcohol-free beer, as he was driving. By 9:30 p.m., they had finished their coffee and were ready to leave. Booth paid for them both while Kirkby went to the bathroom to freshen up.

On the way back out to Rosslare there was a certain amount of sexual tension in the air. Both of them were wondering what might yet come to pass that evening. Kirkby was feeling quite mellow after the wine and the excellent meal, but she was afraid to expect too much from the remainder of the night.

When they pulled up outside her house, Peter switched off the engine and leaned across and kissed Kirkby softly on the lips. A dart of electricity went through her as she responded warmly.

"Coffee?" she said, when they had disengaged.

"Yes, that would be lovely."

They went inside, and while Kirkby busied herself preparing real coffee in the machine, Booth went to the bathroom. When he came back, he sidled up behind her, put his arms around her, and gently kissed the side of her neck. With all thoughts of coffee abandoned, Kirkby led her date upstairs.

* * *

Kirkby awoke at 7:30 the following morning. The bed beside her was empty, and it took her a few moments to focus on what had been an idyllic night of intimacy with Peter Booth. She slipped out of bed, wrapping a thin dressing gown around her, and found a note on the floor by the door.

> *Sorry I had to leave. I couldn't disturb you; you were sleeping so peacefully. I'll call you later. Peter xxxx*

Kirkby smiled and headed for the shower. Could this really have happened? Did she just spend the night with the man who had been every girl's heart-throb at school?

She couldn't stop smiling to herself as she prepared to leave for the station.

Chapter Sixteen

Forty minutes later, and Kirkby was back to reality with a bump. As soon as she had logged onto her PC, she called Cathal Waters into her office. The first thing she noticed about her detective sergeant was that he was looking smarter. He had a new, navy suit which fitted him well, polished black leather shoes, and he'd had his hair cut short. Perhaps a little too short for Kirkby's liking, but she had to admit that the new image was, overall, a lot better.

"Hi, Cathal. Come in. Take the weight off. You're looking well," she said, keen to acknowledge the not-inconsiderable effort the man had made with his appearance.

Waters gave a kind of grunt, and sat down.

"Right, so listen up, Cathal. Here's what I want to do…" Kirkby went on to outline her plan to get to the bottom of the Roches' killings.

Waters looked at her slightly bemused.

"Don't you think it's a bit risky, boss?"

"Perhaps. But we've got bugger all else to go on. But listen, I don't want Superintendent Frawley to get wind of any of this till it's over. He'd probably put a spanner in the works, and then we'd be back to square one. So, let's keep this just between Ciara, you and me, OK?"

"Cripes, you do believe in living dangerously, don't you?" Waters said.

Kirkby picked up on the vibe. He was probably thinking of what the outcome for himself might be if her plan went badly wrong.

"Don't worry, Cathal. If this doesn't work out, it's on me. I'll make sure you're protected. Ciara too. Now, scoot. I have a few phone calls to make."

When Waters had left the office, Kirkby called Peter Booth.

"Hello, you!" he said. "Look, I'm sorry about this morning, but I had to get to work."

"No worries. I understand, anyway, your note was sweet. Listen, I'm looking for some information, Peter. Can you check with the ferry companies and see when the next ship is due in with a few Tiverton Transport wagons on it?"

"OK. But I'm fairly sure that will be the early boat from Fishguard tomorrow. They usually use that one. It gets in here at about 5:30 a.m. They like it, cos it gives the drivers a full day on the road to deliver their stuff."

"Cool. But could you just check it to be certain, and call me back."

"Yes, no problem. Are you free later?" he asked.

"No, not tonight, I'm afraid. But maybe tomorrow."

"OK. I'll call you back."

"Thanks."

The next call she made was to Gerry Healy, the contact Peter had given her for Customs and Excise in Rosslare. It took a little time to locate the man, as he was out on the harbour supervising the arrival of a vessel from France, but he called her back after about an hour.

"Hello, Inspector Kirkby. I believe you were looking for me. How can I help?"

Kirkby outlined her plan which she said she wanted to provisionally put in place for the following morning.

"Well, it's a bit short notice, Inspector. But if it's important, I'm sure we can get it together. When will you be able to confirm?" Healy said.

"Later this morning, but I thought it best to call you to put you on notice, as it were."

"Yes, yes it was. Well look, I'll get busy and see what I can arrange. Let me know as soon as you have a positive confirmation."

"Yes, of course. Thanks, Mr Healy."

"Oh, call me Gerry, Inspector. Everyone does."

It was just after eleven o'clock when Peter Booth called back with the information Kirkby was looking for.

"Hi, it's me. Yes. Tomorrow's early sailing from Fishguard has two Tiverton trucks on it with mixed cargo – mostly fresh stuff like fruit and veg."

"Great. And what time did you say it docks?" Kirkby said.

"Usually at half past five on the button. The forecast is more or less calm, so there shouldn't be any delay. I can get Fishguard to send me a text when it's off the berth if you like?" Booth said.

"Would you mind? Then you can text me so we can get the troops moving."

"Sure, no bother. Or I could come over, and then I could just tell you."

"No. Not tonight, Peter. I'm not trying to play hard to get. It's just that I have to keep my wits about me," Kirkby said.

"Oh, right. Understood. Catch you later then."

"Yes, bye for now."

Kirkby called Gerry Healy and told him that it was 'game on' as she described it, and he told her he would set things up as best he could at short notice.

"I might be able to get a dog unit down from Dublin too. That would make things a whole lot easier for us all," Healy said.

"Great. Thanks, Gerry. I really appreciate it. I'll make sure the paperwork is in order."

* * *

Later in the day Kirkby called Ciara Nestor and Cathal Waters into her office. She explained the plan for the following morning.

"We need as many uniformed officers as we can get our hands on, folks. And we need to be out there at about five o'clock to be ready in case the ship arrives early. I've lined the whole thing up with Customs. They'll have plenty of manpower on hand, and they may even manage a dog unit, so let's be sure everything is ready."

"What exactly are we looking for, boss?" Ciara Nestor asked.

"I'm not sure, Ciara. But something tells me that there's something unsavoury about those Tiverton trucks. My best guess would be drugs. But who knows, it could be anything."

"So, what exactly are we going to do, boss?" Waters asked.

"We wait for the Tiverton trucks to disembark. They'll probably park together in the compound, and when the drivers go inside to collect the clearance cert that they need to get out of the harbour, we'll surround the trailers and open them up. Then we'll search both trailers thoroughly, and hopefully find out if anything is going on," Kirkby said.

"And what if we find nothing, boss?" Waters asked.

"Then I'm in the soup, Cathal. But I don't think that will happen. Frank Roche had highlighted those cargoes for a reason, and my guess is that's what got him and his poor wife killed. So, are we all set? Let's rendezvous outside the pub in Tagoat at five tomorrow. That will give us time to get down to the port before the ship arrives. OK?"

The two Gardaí nodded, but Waters, in particular, looked uncomfortable.

* * *

At 3:10 the following morning, Vikki Kirkby's phone pinged on her bedside locker. She wasn't in a sound sleep in any case, so she reached quickly out and read the message.

Ferry left Fishguard on time. Due Rosslare 05:30.
Peter xxxx

She typed the single word reply 'Thanks' and pressed send.

Chapter Seventeen

When Kirkby and the team arrived at the harbour at 5:15 a.m., it was already bright. There seemed to be an entire army of people in yellow high-vis outfits milling around, and she noticed that a small white van was parked over by the quay wall with 'Customs and Excise, Dog Unit' painted on the side of it.

As Kirkby got out of her car, a man in full Customs uniform approached.

"Good morning, Inspector. I'm Gerry Healy. Good to meet you," he said, extending his hand. Healy was a man in his late forties or early fifties. He was about five foot eleven inches in height, and was quite stocky, without being obese. He had a round, friendly face, and well-trimmed hair going grey at the temples which was just visible under his peaked cap.

"Hello, Gerry. Thanks for arranging this for me. I hope it wasn't too much trouble," Kirkby said.

"It won't be if we find anything," Healy said.

Kirkby outlined her plan to the man who agreed with it and suggested that most of the officers should stay out of sight till the drivers had gone indoors, so as not to spook them.

At 5:25 the ferry, pushing a white bow wave in front of it, entered the harbour between the two granite piers. The water was churned up as the captain skilfully manoeuvred his ship alongside the berth, and sailors on the bow and stern threw heavy ropes across to others waiting on the quayside to tie the ferry up. When the ship had come to rest with its bow doors gaping wide, the hydraulic ramp that would allow the vehicles to drive off was lowered to the sound of claxons. Minutes later, cars began to drive off the ship. Most just drove straight out of the compound, and these were followed by the heavy goods vehicles.

Some fifteen minutes later, the first gleaming white lorry with 'Tiverton Transport' emblazoned across the front of the tractor unit above the windscreen appeared, rapidly followed by a second vehicle in the same livery. They rolled down the ramp, and parked side by side in the compound as predicted. The two drivers climbed down from their cabs and walked into the building to retrieve their documentation. When they were safely inside, Kirkby spoke into her radio.

"Go, go!"

The teams in yellow jackets descended on the rear doors of the two trailers that they were targeting. The lead customs officer snipped the seals on the huge doors, lifted the handles, and opened them, folding them back against the sides of the trailers. In a well-rehearsed move, another officer brought up a forklift truck and started to remove the pallets which were stacked high with coloured plastic crates of fruit and vegetables held in place by cling film wrapping.

As room was created in the load area of the first trailer, the dog handler approached with his energetic springer spaniel dashing here and there, wagging its tail furiously. He directed the animal towards the open trailer, and the dog hopped up, sniffing enthusiastically at the remaining cargo. The dog scampered deeper into the dark void of the container. As this was underway, another customs officer opened the second trailer and the forklift truck unloaded a few more pallets onto the concrete yard.

Several minutes passed with the dog and the men doing their rummaging inside the chilled wagons. Then, the two drivers emerged from the office block and walked over to where their vehicles were being plundered.

"What the fuck is going on here?" shouted the first man in a strong English accent. He marched in a determined fashion towards the gaping rear of his truck.

Kirkby spotted him at once and intercepted him before he got to the trailer.

"Wait there, please, sir. Are you the driver of this wagon?" she said.

"I am. And who the fuck are you?" he shouted, bringing his face close to Kirkby's.

"Step back, please, sir. My name is Detective Inspector Vikki Kirkby from the Wexford Detective Unit," she said, holding up her warrant card, "what's your name?"

"Never mind that. What's going on here?" the driver said, calming down a little.

"We're inspecting your vehicle, that's all. No need to go all Rambo on me. We suspect there may be some contraband inside. It's all above board. I have a warrant here if you would like to see it," she said, walking the man backwards away from the vehicle being searched. "Now, I need your name and identity papers please."

"Andy Brooks, and my stuff is in the cab. But I'll tell you, you're wasting your time. There ain't no contraband on my wagon, that's for sure."

"Well, we shall see. I'd like you to wait over there by the Garda car until we have finished. What's the other driver's name?"

"You'd better ask him, hadn't you," Brooks said in a grumpy fashion.

"I'm asking you, Mr Brooks, and if I were you, I'd be careful. This is no time to be a smart-arse," Kirkby said, a little surprised at her own demeanour. But this guy was bringing out the worst in her.

"Tommy. Tommy Miller. You going to arrest him and all?"

"That depends on what we find. Now why don't you go and wait over there," she said, indicating where the marked Garda cars were parked.

Brooks slumped off, clearly feeling very hard done by.

Kirkby walked over to where Cathal Waters was having a similar conversation with Tommy Miller.

"Everything OK, Sergeant?" she said.

"Yes, boss. Mr Miller here is just telling me that there's no chance that there's anything dodgy in the wagons, and if there is, they know nothing about it."

With that, Miller chimed in, "That's right. We don't know nothing about any funny stuff."

"Well, check his ID, license and tachograph, and then put him over there with the other fellow," she said. "I'm going to see how the search is going."

Gerry Healy was standing at the back of one of the open lorries talking to another customs officer.

"Hi, Gerry. Anything?"

Healy put his hand on Kirkby's elbow and led her away a few metres, out of earshot of the other man.

"I'm sorry to tell you, Inspector, but I think these two wagons are clean. We've had the dog in both of them, and she found nothing. Not a whiff. And we've searched through several of the pallets, and it all looks fine."

"Shit! What is the dog trained to find?"

"Well, obviously drugs, but she'd react to weapons, or a large quantity of cash too. No, I'm sorry, it looks like just a whole pile of fruit and veg," Healy said.

"Christ, that's all I bloody need. How much longer will you be?"

"About another half an hour. We have to put it all back the way we found it and seal them up again."

"What about the two drivers?" Kirkby said.

"Ah, don't mind them. My lads will sort them out. It's an occupational hazard for them getting stopped and examined. Happens all the time. We'll buy them a cup of tea and a bun and they'll be fine."

"Thanks, Gerry. Sorry about this. Our information was obviously wrong. And are you sure there's nothing in the cabs?"

"Yes, certain. But what exactly were you hoping to find, anyway?" Healy said.

"Anything that could have got Frank Roche killed, that's all."

Kirkby left the man to finish up with his officers reloading the trucks and speaking to the drivers. She found Cathal Waters nursing a cardboard cup of coffee, standing by her car.

"What's the story, boss?"

"There isn't one, Cathal. Nada! Zippo!"

"Hmm… OK. What are we going to do now then?"

"Back to the station, I guess. I'm not looking forward to that!"

Chapter Eighteen

Kirkby sat uneasily in the chair in front of Superintendent Frawley's desk. He was poring over a small stack of papers, ticking and signing here and there. He had made no eye contact with Kirkby since she entered the room, and had issued just a single word to her, which was 'sit'.

More minutes went past excruciatingly slowly as the tension between the two of them built. Eventually, Frawley tapped his papers into a neat bundle, put them aside and looked up.

"Well, Inspector, maybe you'd like to tell me why you arranged that circus out at the port this morning without informing me in advance. I gather it was a complete waste of time!"

"Not entirely, sir. At least we proved that Tiverton Transport aren't smuggling drugs or anything else through Rosslare."

"Is that it? Having cost the force God knows how much in wasted resources, and made us look like complete fools with the customs people, not to mention the backdraught we will get from the transport company, is that seriously all you have to show for your little dog and pony show?"

"My decision to set up the search of the lorries was based on strong evidence, sir. I know we didn't find anything, and that's regrettable, but I still think it was worth doing," Kirkby said.

"Do you? And has it occurred to you that if there is anything iffy going on with this Tiverton lot, you have just about ensured that they'll change their modus operandi immediately, making sure that we don't discover whatever they are up to, if anything."

"I still think it was worth the gamble, sir. Frank Roche had highlighted that company in his paperwork. Several trips had been marked up, and I'm certain that he did that for a good reason. And after all, someone didn't like whatever he was up to very much."

"Look, Inspector, when you arrived here from Dublin, I was prepared to give you a chance. Yes, you came with a bit of a reputation for screwing things up, but that may or may not have been all your fault. How should I know? But I was prepared to give you the benefit of the doubt. And now see what's happened. You've not only made us all look like right eejits, but my judgement could well be called into question for trusting you too. And don't forget, you're supposed to be solving a double murder. I don't suppose there's any good news on that front?"

"We're following a few lines of enquiry, sir."

"In other words, no! Here's what we're going to do. Just in case there is the remotest chance that you can recover this position, I'm going to give you another forty-eight hours on the case. If you haven't made significant progress in that time, then I'm handing it over to Jim Kennedy and his team, and you can take some sick leave till all this blows over. Understood?"

"But I'm not unwell, sir."

"Don't be naive, Vikki. You know exactly what I mean. Now get out of my sight before I change my mind."

* * *

When Kirkby got back downstairs to the open-plan, Cathal Waters and Ciara Nestor were both at Nestor's desk chatting. Waters was perched on the edge of the desk, and Nestor was seated, facing out into the room.

"How did that go, boss?" Waters ventured when he saw Kirkby.

"Just peachy, Cathal. The boss is going to get me a commendation for being the stupidest Garda inspector in the force, and I have to give up my pay for the next fifty years to cover the cost of our little adventure. No, seriously, he was livid. But he's letting us get on with it, for now. Anything here?"

Ciara Nestor piped up, "I dunno, boss. I've been going back over the paperwork we got from Frank Roche's shed. There's something not right, but I can't put my finger on it. Not yet, in any case."

"Give us a clue, Ciara. We need something, and soon," Kirkby said.

"I need to do some more analysis. It definitely revolves around that Tiverton outfit, but I can't see what it is. Not yet anyway."

"Right, then. I want both of you to get to work on that. Analyse it to death till you find whatever's bothering you, Ciara, and let me know as soon as you get anything. I'm heading out for a while. I have some thinking to do."

"Right, boss. See you later."

* * *

Kirkby got into her car and set off. She drove out towards Rosslare, but when she got to Tagoat, she turned off and took the R736 towards Tomhaggard. As she passed the Wexford Equestrian Centre, she turned left again onto the R739 and drove on to the end of that road at Kilmore Quay.

Kilmore Quay had expanded a great deal since she was a child going to school in Wexford. On some Sundays, after mass, her parents would take a picnic in their old Ford Cortina and drive out to the place with Kirkby and her brother fighting in the back for most of the journey. When they arrived at their destination, which was no more than a couple of cottages and a small harbour, they would set off walking in a westerly direction along Ballyteige Burrow, until they found a sheltered spot between the dunes. Then, Kirkby's mother would spread out a large chequered woollen rug on the ground, and unpack the picnic basket containing sandwiches and home-made cake, while her father wrestled with the camping stove to boil water for tea. The blessed thing rarely worked, but the entire ritual was all part of the fun. If it was warm enough, Kirkby and her brother would go for a swim to work up an appetite, splashing around on the gently sloping sands.

She parked her car, got out and went for a walk to try and clear her head, and work through how things had got to where they were, and what she might now do to improve matters. She was in deep trouble with Frawley, and she couldn't afford to slip up any further, or she would be busted down to an ordinary uniformed Garda and posted to God knows where. She was strolling along, deep in thought, when her phone rang. It was Peter Booth.

"Hi. What's up?" she said.

"Hi. I just thought I'd give you a call. You're quite the celebrity out here today! How are things?"

"Ha ha, very funny. You know how things are – shit!"

"That good, eh? Well, let me cheer you up. How about a nice romantic dinner with me tonight. I'll book somewhere cosy."

"Sounds like just what a girl needs to take her mind off things. What time?" she said.

"I'll collect you at eight, if that's OK?"

"Yes, fine. Thanks, Peter."

"See ya!" he said, and rang off.

Kirkby walked on for another half a mile out along the sandy shore, listening to the waves gently lapping on the golden sand. She wondered how far things would go with Booth as well. She was falling for him a little more quickly than felt comfortable, but she needed something positive in her life after all that she had been through. But was he the right one to deliver it?

"Ah, to hell with it," she said to herself, "you only live once!" And she turned and walked back to the car with more of a spring in her step.

Chapter Nineteen

Peter Booth arrived at Kirkby's house at exactly 8 p.m. She had spent quite some time making herself presentable, and had dabbed a small amount of very expensive Jo Malone perfume behind her ears and on the inside of her wrists. She glanced in the mirror close to the front door before opening it.

"You'll do," she said to herself, and few would have disagreed.

Booth greeted her with a warm smile.

"You look amazing, Vikki. I'm a lucky guy," he said, advancing on her and giving her a gentle kiss, his arm around her shoulders.

"Easy, tiger. We don't want the neighbours gossiping. Not too much anyway. Where are we off to?"

"I've booked that French fish restaurant on the quays in town. OK with you?"

"Yes, great, but it's very expensive. Can we go Dutch?"

"Let's sort that out later. But I hope you're hungry," Booth said as he opened the car door for her.

* * *

Thirty minutes later they were seated at a quiet table in one corner of the restaurant. The place wasn't full, but there were a number of other couples enjoying the hospitality, and one table of ten that were making a bit more noise. They studied the extensive menu in silence, and when Kirkby had made her selection, she put it down on the white linen tablecloth.

"What are you going to have, Vikki?" Booth enquired.

"I'm a simple girl really. I'll start with a few mussels, and then I'll go for the monkfish. I like the sound of the sauce. What about you?"

"That sounds like an excellent choice. I hope you don't mind if I copy you," Booth said.

"Of course not."

At that moment a waitress appeared with a large basket of varied bread items, and offered it to them both in turn. Kirkby chose a small brown roll, while Booth went for a generous slice of sourdough.

When the waitress had taken their order and departed, Booth said, "So, how are things going with your murder case?"

"Oh, don't, will you? After that little performance out at the port, I'm not exactly flavour of the month. I have a definite feeling that there's something going on with those Tiverton trucks, and I was sure we'd find some-bloody-thing in one of those wagons. I don't suppose you've heard anything? We might have stirred up a bit of gossip with the search and all the fuss."

"No, 'fraid not. There is a bit of smuggling going on through the port. We all know that, and the lads pounce from time to time and catch a load of tobacco or drugs, but I don't think it's very widespread. Anyway, I'm more concerned with scheduling the ferries on and off the berths and making sure the place is safe and secure. We had a car full of nuns that almost went into the harbour earlier this year. Nearly gave me a heart attack!" Booth said.

Kirkby couldn't help but laugh a little.

"Crikey! How did that happen?"

"They were coming off the ferry and misjudged the gap between the ramp and the pier. Two wheels of their car went over the edge, and of course got stuck."

"Were they OK?"

"Yes, eventually. They got an awful fright. But we got them out on the high side, and then a few of the boys lifted the car back onto terra firma. No extra charge!"

"Terrific. I bet that story kept the pubs busy for a few nights. But listen, I still think there may be something iffy about those Tiverton lorries. When will there be any more of them coming in?" Kirkby said.

The waitress arrived at the table with two steaming bowls of mussels giving off a delicious aroma of a mixture of sea, garlic and white wine. Another waiter brought the bottle of chardonnay that Booth had ordered, and he went through the ritual of tasting it, before nodding to the man who poured two generous measures into their glasses.

When the servers had departed, Booth said, "I'm not sure, but I could find out if you like. What are you planning to do?"

"If I told you that, I'd have to shoot you! Just kidding. But seriously, just let me know when they are expected and then pretend you know nothing about it," Kirkby said.

"Sounds ominous. OK, I'll find out tomorrow and let you know."

As they ate the rest of their delicious meal, they conversed about the long interval after they had both left school until they met again recently. Booth was particularly interested in Kirkby's adventures with the Dublin Gardaí, and she was able to regale him with some pretty sordid stories of her time in the capital.

"Are you finding it very dull being back after all that high drama?" Booth said.

"No, not at all. I've had more drama in the last week than I can handle, and it's not over yet. Don't forget we still have a double murderer to find."

"Yes, it must be very difficult. I can't imagine what it must be like to lead a murder enquiry," he responded, though probably not really understanding her situation at all.

They finished their dinner, and when the bill arrived Kirkby made a genuine effort to pay her share, but Booth would hear none of it.

"You can get me next time," he said, smiling, and handing his bank card to the waitress.

Kirkby noticed that he added a generous tip to the total, earning a broad smile and a big 'thank you' from the woman who was clearly delighted.

Booth drove them back out to Rosslare Strand. The evening tide had caused the wind to drop to a whisper, and it was a delightful summer evening, not really dark, although the hour was late.

When they got to Kirkby's front door, Booth said, "Am I coming in?"

"Do you want to?" Kirkby replied.

"Of course."

She still couldn't believe her luck in becoming intimate with her school heart-throb, but she wasn't complaining.

Chapter Twenty

At nine o'clock the following morning, Kirkby brought Cathal Waters and Ciara Nestor into her office.

"Right, team, we have just two days to make some serious progress with this case, or it's going to be taken off our hands, and that won't go well for any of us. So, we need to get on and make some headway, preferably today. Cathal, have you any fresh ideas?"

"I was thinking, boss. So far, we have focussed entirely on Mr Roche. I know it's a bit of a long shot, but could it be that the woman was actually the intended victim all along? We haven't really investigated her at all," Waters said.

"Hmm... interesting. If only for the sake of thoroughness, maybe you should go out to her workplace and speak to her colleagues. See if there's anything odd there. I think someone said she worked part-time in the school at Wellingtonbridge."

"Yes, that's right. I'll go out there this morning and see what I can find out," Waters said.

Kirkby noted that the man was still looking smarter than he had been when she first met him, and now he was coming up with ideas all on his own. Things were improving!

"What about you, Ciara? Anything?" Kirkby said.

"I'm still analysing the paperwork from Frank Roche's shed. There's loads of it. I may be onto something, but I'm not saying till I've done some more work. Have you any ideas, boss?"

"I'm still uneasy about those Tiverton trucks, but after yesterday's little performance, I'd better go easy. Frawley was hopping mad. I'm going to do a bit more digging here.

Oh, by the way, did we bring in the Roches' vehicle? I think it was parked at the back of the house in the laneway."

Waters and Nestor looked at each other blankly.

"I take it that's a 'no' then. Ciara, can you get onto transport and get them to fetch it in. I want forensics to go over it in case there's anything of interest," Kirkby said.

"Eh... we don't really have a transport section, boss. We usually use a local garage with a tow-truck," Nestor said.

"Christ! OK, well then get forensics to organise it. We don't want greasy paw prints all over the damn thing contaminating any possible evidence."

"Right, boss. I'll get onto it when we're finished here."

"Have either of you anything more on our elusive Spaniard, Hernandez?"

Waters and Nestor looked blankly from one to the other.

"Terrific! Look, guys, we need to up the energy a bit here. Cathal, can you follow up on that? Check the airports and the ferry ports. See if he has been coming and going recently and let's see if we can't run the bugger to earth. He has to be somewhere. Right, well that's all we can do for now. Let's meet again at five o'clock for an update."

When the meeting was over, Ciara Nestor came back into Kirkby's office.

"Sorry, boss. Superintendent Frawley is looking for you," she said.

"Fantastic! Thanks, Ciara."

* * *

Kirkby trooped up the stairs to the top floor where the superintendent had his spacious, and quite luxurious office, with a heavy heart. Given the way things had been going, he was probably gunning for her again. She knocked firmly on his door, and from inside, she heard him say, "Come."

"Ah, Inspector, come in, take a seat."

Kirkby did as she was told and sat nervously at the edge of her chair.

"Inspector," the superintendent said looking her directly in the eyes, "information has been given to me that you are associating socially with one Peter Booth. Is that correct?"

"Where did you get that from, sir?"

"Don't play games with me, Inspector. Is it true or not?"

"Peter and I have been out a couple of times, yes, sir."

"Are you out of your tiny mind, Inspector?" Frawley said, getting a little red around the face.

"How do you mean, sir?"

"Booth is, as I understand it, some sort of officer in the Rosslare Europort company. And there you are arranging raids on lorries coming in through the port – why I can only imagine – and dating someone who could quite possibly be a person of interest in a double murder case. Is this how they taught you to behave in Dublin?" Frawley said, getting redder.

"I can assure you that Peter Booth is by no means a suspect in that regard, sir, and in–" Kirkby said, somewhat lost for words.

"Can you now?" Frawley interrupted, "and what would that assurance be based upon, may I ask? Woman's intuition!"

Kirkby didn't reply. She was livid. How dare he bring her gender into the discussion like that.

"Well?" Frawley said.

"Sir, you have given me forty-eight hours to see if I can make real progress in this case, and I intend to use it wisely and by whatever means I can to demonstrate my ability as a detective. I'd be obliged if you would allow me to get on with the task in hand."

"I see. Very well. I did give you two days, and I'm a man of my word. But rest assured when that time has elapsed, we will be having a further discussion about your judgement, or lack of it, and you may not like what I have to say."

Kirkby said nothing. She simply got up and left the room.

* * *

On her way back down to her office, Kirkby's mobile phone rang. She could see from the caller ID that it was Peter Booth.

"Hi. What's up?"

"Hi to you too. You asked when Tiverton will have another vehicle on the inbound ferry. There's one due in at one o'clock, and they have a chilled wagon on board. Just one this time. Is that any good?"

"Yes, thanks Peter, that's great."

"What have you in mind, Vikki?"

"Ah, don't worry, nothing that involves you in any case. But thanks for the information."

"You're welcome. Are you free later?"

Kirkby remembered the dressing-down she had endured from her superintendent a few minutes earlier.

"No, not tonight. I'll call you. OK?"

"Yes, OK. Is everything all right?"

"Just peachy. Now, I gotta go. Talk soon. Bye."

Kirkby looked at her watch. She would just have time to get back out to the port at Rosslare before the ferry docked. She headed for her car.

* * *

It was overcast, and looked as if it could rain, as Kirkby drove out along the N25 towards the harbour. The wind had got up too, and as she rounded the last bend before the road that led steeply downhill towards the port, she could see that there were white caps on the waves out in the open sea.

Kirkby turned her car around, and parked at the side of the road near the exit from the Customs yard so that she was facing back the way she had come. The ferry had berthed and vehicles of every description were disgorging from the gaping bow door. After what seemed like an eternity, she finally saw the Tiverton rig lumbering across the ramp and stopping in the lorry park while the driver went indoors to complete formalities.

Twenty minutes later, the Tiverton lorry emerged from the yard, its engine whining and grinding as the truck made its way up the hill, passing Kirkby's car as it did so. Kirkby started her engine and allowed one or two other cars to go past her before she moved off keeping a close eye on the large white Tiverton refrigerated trailer.

Chapter Twenty-One

Keeping a discreet distance from the vehicle she was following, Kirkby found herself travelling along the Clonard Road back in Wexford. When they got to the Westpoint Business Park, the Tiverton lorry turned in, and stopped outside a large, single-storey unit with a sign depicting 'Wexford Fruit and Veg — Wholesale Only' above the steel roller doors. The Tiverton lorry backed up skilfully to the loading bay, and the rear doors were opened.

From where Kirkby was parked outside the industrial estate, she couldn't see all that was going on, but she guessed that the trailer was being unloaded. She shifted her position, and could then make out a forklift truck going into the trailer and fetching pallets of fruit similar to the ones that they had encountered during the abortive raid on the previous day.

After around thirty minutes, the driver pulled the rig clear of the loading bay, got out to close the back doors, and then climbed back into his cab and set off. Kirkby followed at a safe distance.

She was travelling at a steady 50 kph a couple of cars back from her quarry when her phone rang. She answered using the Bluetooth remote in her car.

"Kirkby," she said.

"Hello, Inspector, it's Keith here from forensics. I'm ringing about Frank Roche's van. We recovered it from the back of his place earlier, and I've been examining it."

"Oh, great, Keith. Anything?"

"Yes, there is actually. In the back, under some old sacks, we found a few square, yellow vehicle number plates. They look like UK ones."

"I see. How many are there?"

"Just four. What do you want me to do with them?" Keith asked.

"Could you call Ciara Nestor at the station and give her the numbers? Tell her I asked if she could check them with the UK authorities and see what they belong to."

"Yes, OK," Keith said.

"Was there anything else of interest in the van, Keith?"

"Nothing so far, but we're not finished with it yet. I'll let you know if we find anything else."

"OK. Thanks. Bye."

Kirkby continued to follow the Tiverton truck. It made a further stop at another wholesale fruit and vegetable merchants, and this time, she could observe the unloading process clearly. By the time the process was complete, the trailer was completely empty. Kirkby wanted to stick with the lorry. She expected that it would either go back towards the port, or in a different direction altogether to collect a backload, if there was one available. So, she wasn't surprised when it turned out of the yard going in the opposite direction. She followed it, but had to hang back quite a bit as there was no traffic and she didn't want to be seen by the driver. After a few miles of twisty roads, they both turned onto the N25, travelling away from Wexford. Kirkby didn't know the area very well. She hadn't been a driver when she left the town all those years ago, and her knowledge of the county was confined to Wexford itself, and its immediate hinterland.

When they had gone about fifteen kilometres, the truck indicated left, and turned onto the R735 towards Newbawn. They passed through Newbawn crossroads with its old defunct petrol station, and then the lorry swung in suddenly to the right, onto a very narrow single-track laneway. Kirkby had to brake hard to avoid running into the back of the vehicle, and then she drove on a little way and pulled her car into a gateway where she stopped the motor and got out. She could still see the roof of the articulated truck progressing along the lane at quite some speed, the top of the container brushing against the foliage of the trees that lined the ditches to the sides.

Kirkby listened carefully, and after a few moments, she detected the change in engine noise of the lorry as the driver shifted down through the gears. Then she heard the revving of a heavy diesel engine, telling her that it was being manoeuvred in a tight space, before it finally cut out altogether with a loud hiss of pneumatic brakes.

Kirkby stepped across the road and into a field through the hedge, hiding her presence from the road. She hunched down making sure that she was well out of sight, and waited. After another few minutes, she could hear the sound of another, smaller, vehicle coming back down the laneway. She took a chance, and stood up, hoping that the undergrowth would camouflage her presence sufficiently, and saw a green Ford Escort van approaching with the man that she recognised as the driver of the truck in the passenger's seat. The van barely stopped at the junction and then sped off from the direction Kirkby had come from.

Kirkby crept silently up along the ditch on the field side of the lane. As she moved froward, she could see that the lane opened into a large yard, and there was a modern-looking shed of enormous proportions taking up about half of the entire space. Outside the shed stood several three-axle lorry trailers, all freshly painted and looking like new, while the noise of men at work came from inside.

Kirkby crept further up along the field and into the next one so that she could get a better look at whatever was going on. She managed to position herself so that she had quite a good view into the barn, the doors of which were standing open.

The interior of the cavernous shed was quite well lit, and there was a sort of gantry standing up against a trailer just like the one she had been following. A man – at least she assumed it was a man – dressed in a one-piece blue coverall, and with a full mask and filter on his face, was spray-painting the side of the refrigerated rig in plain white. The wheels and undercarriage of the trailer had been masked off with old sacks, to protect them from getting covered in overspray. Kirkby got the smell of cellulose paint in the air as it wafted across from the yard. She took out her phone, and carefully captured a few frames of the operation and the trailers standing outside in the yard.

Kirkby didn't know what to do. She could call for back-up, but what she had seen could easily be a perfectly legitimate operation, in which case, she would look ridiculous again in front of the team, and Superintendent Frawley in particular. She wasn't ready for that. She decided to wait where she was for a while. It was approaching five o'clock, and she thought that work at the yard might stop soon and the place would empty out. She hunkered down against the hedge and waited, wishing that she had brought a bar of chocolate or a sandwich with her. She was ravenous.

Kirkby was getting stiff and cold after nearly an hour sitting on the damp ground when she finally heard the sound of voices, and the noise of a huge roller shutter being let down to the ground. There was some chat and laughter coming from the yard, and then the distinctive noise of car doors slamming. Kirkby peeked over the hedge carefully to see two rather beaten-up cars pulling out of the yard and speeding down the lane throwing up dust and gravel as they departed. An eerie silence descended on the place.

Chapter Twenty-Two

St Mary's school was a modest establishment that occupied a Victorian manor house set in its own grounds on the R736. The house had presumably, at some stage, stood in many acres of land, but these days it had just enough to accommodate a games pitch, a tennis court and a front lawn, all of which were immaculately tended. The curved, gravelled driveway led to a generous area before the front door which had steps up to it and a granite portico.

Waters parked beside a smart-looking red Alfa Romeo which was one of six cars outside the school's entrance. He got out and went into the building. Inside the hallway, the floor of which was covered in black and white diamond-shaped tiles, there were three highly polished mahogany doors and a cantilevered staircase with a metal balustrade leading to the upper floors. The door in the centre of the three bore the word 'Office' in gold lettering. He walked over and knocked on the door, and opened it, entering the room.

Inside there were three desks arranged in a horseshoe shape, and a large window with small glass panes that looked out onto the games pitch. Bookcases, filled with a variety of scholarly works, adorned the walls, and a few visitors' chairs made with dark wooden frames and brown Rexine seat covers on ceramic castors stood about. A woman of middle age, with tight grey curls and dressed in a green suit, occupied the desk facing the door.

"Good morning. My name is Detective Sergeant Cathal Waters from the Wexford police. And you are…?" he said.

"Kitty Malone. How can I help you, Sergeant?"

Waters was still standing awkwardly inside the door, and Malone sensed his discomfort.

"Please, take a seat," she said, gesturing to one of the chairs.

"Thanks. I understand Mrs Eileen Roche worked with you here at the school. Is that correct?"

Malone, who was the only other occupant of the room, took a tissue from her sleeve and dabbed her nose.

"Yes. Eileen worked here with us in this very room, Sergeant. Have you discovered what happened to them? We've never heard of anything like this around here."

"Our investigation is ongoing, Ms Malone. May I ask what exactly Mrs Roche did here at the school?" Waters said.

"Eileen looked after the accounts for us. She did our payroll; paid suppliers; looked after our donations and the money we get from the department. To be frank, we're lost without her."

"I see. May I ask if the school has the accounts audited, Ms Malone?"

"Yes, of course. Why? You can't think that Eileen's death had anything to do with the school, surely?"

"Was there ever any comment made on the accounts at all?"

"No. Never. Everything was always perfectly in order. Eileen was very thorough," Kitty Malone said.

"Have you noticed anyone odd hanging around the school lately? Anyone you don't know, or anyone new calling frequently to the school?"

"No. Nothing like that, Sergeant. But why are you interested in Eileen's work? What's going on?"

"We have to investigate everything in these cases, Ms Malone. As you know, both Mr and Mrs Roche were shot at their home. Anything that could be in any way relevant has to be looked into. May I ask if Mrs Roche had control of the school's bank account?"

"Yes, of course she did. She signed all the cheques that we send out, and did the transfers for the staff at the end of the month. Look, Sergeant, I'm not sure what you're getting at here, but Eileen Roche was completely trustworthy. She's been here for several years, and there were never any issues. None whatsoever."

"OK, OK, I hear you. I'm sorry, but I have to ask these questions. It's my job. Just one more thing, then I'll leave you alone. Did you notice anything different about Mrs Roche's behaviour lately? Did she seem anxious or worried about anything?"

Malone appeared to think for a moment before answering.

"No, not so that I noticed anyway, and I would have. We were on quite friendly terms, even though she was only part-time."

"OK. Thanks for your time. May I ask which was Eileen Roche's desk?"

"Yes. It was that one," she said, pointing to the desk to Waters' left.

"I don't suppose I could have a look in it?" Waters said, smiling.

"I don't think that would be appropriate, Sergeant. Now if you don't mind, I have work to do."

"Sorry. Yes, of course. I'll leave you to it."

* * *

Cathal Waters left the school and drove back to Wexford. He wondered if he should have perhaps been a little more assertive with Kitty Malone. But he didn't have a search warrant, and he doubted if there was anything in Eileen Roche's desk that would explain why she was so brutally murdered in any case. When he got back to the office, Ciara Nestor asked him to come across to her desk to have a look at something.

"Thanks, Sarge. I don't want to bother the boss if this is nothing, but could you have a look at this with me and tell me I'm not going bonkers."

"Sure. What have you got?"

Ciara Nestor showed Waters the spreadsheet that she had prepared and explained what she thought she had discovered.

"Cripes! I think you're right, Ciara. The boss will be very interested in this, that's for sure. Where is she anyway?"

"I don't know. She went out earlier."

"Well as soon as she's back, put her in the picture. Well done you," Waters said.

"Thanks."

Chapter Twenty-Three

Kirkby waited for a further half-hour before stirring from her hideout. The place had been totally silent, save for the sound of birds and the occasional distant barking of a farmyard dog. She got up and moved along the ditch that ran at the back of the compound until she found a place where the fence was damaged, and climbed through. It wasn't easy, but she needed to get up close to the three trailers that were parked outside the huge shed to examine them.

Once inside the yard, she kept to the edges, and crept around until she was leaning up against the wall of the large building. She looked up, and saw that there was a security camera mounted high up at the corner of the workshop but mercifully it was directed at the massive roller shutter that was now closed. She could see no other cameras.

Hunching down to make herself smaller, she crept along the wall until she was directly behind the first trailer. She could get the smell of new cellulose paint from it, and could see that it had been recently refurbished to a high standard. She bent down to look underneath. Strong black chassis rails ran the length of the vehicle, and these too had recently been painted, so that the whole rig looked brand new.

Using the trailer itself for cover, Kirkby crept along its length towards the front where the refrigeration unit was housed. As she advanced, she spotted an identification plate riveted to the chassis. She took out her phone and photographed the details on the tag, noting that 'Year of Manufacture' was shown as the current year. She worked her way further up along, and around the front of the unit, and then back down the other side, observing that it too was in more or less pristine condition. She then did the same with the other two trailers, photographing their registration details as before.

Kirkby was about to walk around the building, making sure to stay out of sight of the cameras, to see if there was a door or a window left open that she could get in by, when she heard a vehicle approaching along the narrow road. She figured it was heading for the yard, as there was nothing much else along the lane. Moments later, crouched down behind the back of the nearest truck, she saw the old green van enter the yard. There were two men in the van, and when it had stopped not thirty metres away from her, they both got out. She recognised one of the men as the driver of the lorry that she had seen earlier at the port.

"I'd better be getting off then," the driver said to his mate. "I don't want to miss the ferry."

"Right enough. When will you be back?" the other man said.

"Probably next week. I should have another one for you then."

"Good stuff. I think I have two of these sold anyway, so we'll be needing another one soon. At the prices we charge, they don't hang about."

The driver walked over to the tractor unit, opened the door, climbed in and started the engine. With no trailer attached, the lorry left the compound briskly, throwing up a small cloud of dust and gravel, and disappeared down the lane.

Kirkby stayed where she was, afraid to move or make a sound for fear of being discovered. The driver of the old green van strolled around the yard tidying up a few old pallets and boxes that were strewn here and there. Kirkby wondered how long he would stay for. She was getting very hungry, and was quite uncomfortable. Just as the man looked as if he was walking back to his van, Kirkby's phone started to ring in her pocket. The man stopped, and cocked an ear, looking around him to try and identify where the noise was coming from. Kirkby acted quickly and silenced the device, praying that it wouldn't give her presence away.

The man looked around the yard again, shrugged his shoulders, and got into his vehicle and drove out of the yard, stopping outside to secure the high metal gates with a stout chain and padlock.

Kirkby waited until she was sure he had actually departed before looking at the screen on her phone. It was Peter Booth calling her, and she cursed herself for being so careless by not turning her phone off before she went snooping. She retraced her steps back through the hole in the fence and out into the field. A few minutes later she was back at her car, thankful to have got away with her adventure undiscovered.

As it was getting late, Kirkby decided not to go all the way back to the Garda station. Instead, she drove towards Rosslare. She passed the turn for Rosslare Strand and drove on towards the port. As she approached the village, she decided to go into the Hotel Rosslare and get something to eat. She had some thinking to do on a number of topics, and she couldn't do that without sustenance inside her.

When she had downed a steak and salad in the excellent restaurant, accompanied by a small glass of red wine, she sat in the lounge over a coffee looking out at the port which was still busy. She saw the tractor unit from Tiverton Transport lined up in the queue waiting to board the Fishguard ship, and she began to put two and two together.

Chapter Twenty-Four

It was a miserable day the following morning. Although it wasn't cold, heavy grey clouds hung over the south-east of Ireland, and persistent rain fell from the sky. As Kirkby looked out of the kitchen window of her rented house in Rosslare Strand, the sea was an angry greeny-grey colour with lots of white horses whipped up by the strong breeze. But the grim weather didn't deter Kirkby from focusing on the matter in hand. She had just one day to make considerable headway in the case of the murder of Eileen and Frank Roche, as otherwise, she was sure, Superintendent Frawley would happily take her off the case. She wasn't about to let that happen.

After a hearty breakfast of scrambled eggs and bacon, accompanied by steaming hot coffee, she donned a waterproof jacket and set off for Wexford.

As soon as she arrived at the station, even before she got into her office, Ciara Nestor caught her attention.

"Sorry, boss, can I have a word?" Nestor said.

"Yes, of course, Ciara. Just give me a chance to get my jacket off," she said, shrugging off her rain-soaked coat and placing it on the back of her office chair.

"I need to show you something on my own PC, boss," Nestor said, clearly finding it difficult to contain her enthusiasm.

Kirkby realised that her colleague must have something important to show her, so she went back out to Nestor's desk without delay.

"OK. What have you got?" she said, leaning over Nestor's shoulder as the woman tapped the keys on her keyboard.

"Right. Well, as you know I've been analysing all that stuff we brought back in from Frank Roche's shed. At first, I couldn't quite make out what I was seeing. But then it came to me," Nestor said.

Kirkby was getting a little impatient with Nestor building up the tension in the way that she was, but she stayed quiet, as she didn't want to burst the junior officer's bubble.

"Look. Here it is," Nestor said using her pen to point to an area of the screen.

"What am I looking at, Ciara?"

"The trucks. Tiverton Transport bring fruit and veg across from England in these refrigerated trailers. But they don't always bring the trailers back. On several occasions, the tractor units return without the trailers, and those trailers never go back at all. Those are the cases that Frank Roche had highlighted on the paperwork."

"I see what you're saying, but that doesn't make sense, unless of course you put it together with what I discovered last night out near Newbawn. I was out there, and found a yard where they appeared to be reconditioning trailers, and one of them was brought in behind a Tiverton lorry," Kirkby said.

"Yes. And that's not all. I did a bit more work on these big fridge trailers. The cost of a new or nearly new one in Ireland is around €57,000 to €60,000. But in the UK, you can buy a one-year-old one for more like £30,000, or even a bit less. Of course, there's VAT to be paid if you bring them over for sale, but if you don't officially import the trailer, you don't have to pay VAT at all. So, you can make twenty to twenty-five grand on each one."

"What would the VAT be on one of those anyway?" Kirkby said.

"It's twenty-three percent of the purchase price, so around €9,000 a pop."

"Cripes! Well done you! It's no wonder we didn't find anything illegal in the trailers the other day. It's not the contents that being smuggled, it's the wagons themselves!"

"Yes. And it looks like Roche was onto them, whoever they are. And they wouldn't like to have such a nice little money-making scheme upset, never mind an almost certain jail sentence for VAT fraud," Nestor said.

"Worth killing for?" Kirkby said.

"Looks like it. Especially if Frank Roche was trying to muscle in on the scam or threaten them with exposure," Nestor said.

"Hmm… looks like thanks to your good work, Ciara, we have our motive. Look, let's get Cathal in and have a briefing. We need to do a bit more work on this before I take it upstairs and try to buy some more time."

* * *

Vikki Kirkby, Cathal Waters and Ciara Nestor all sat around Kirkby's desk in her office.

Nestor had brought Cathal Waters up to speed on her discovery.

"Right. We need to work hard, and work quickly. I want to bring a watertight story up to Frawley after lunch to persuade him to leave the case with us. So, Ciara, have you done anything with those number plates that were found in Frank Roche's van?"

"I'm waiting on a call back from the DVLA in the UK," Nestor said.

"Well, we don't have time to wait. Get back onto them and give them a rattle. We need to know if there's a connection to the trucks. Cathal, I'm going to send you a few photographs of identification tags I snapped last night out at Newbawn. Can you get onto Wexford County

Council and speak to whoever looks after the registration of trailers. Find out if these are legit, and if so, who registered them," Kirkby said.

She took out her phone and forwarded the photos to Waters' phone which pinged as they were received.

"And, Cathal, have you had any luck tracking down Hernandez?" Kirkby said.

"No, boss. Not a sign of him. He hasn't been through any passport controls here, in any case, at least not using his own name. And no one has responded to the photographs we circulated. No one at all," Waters said.

"OK. Well get back onto the Spanish police. Emphasise that he is a person of interest in a murder enquiry here and we would appreciate their cooperation. Push them as hard as you like."

"Right, boss."

"Let's meet back at noon and see how far we've got."

When the two detectives had left her office, Kirkby lifted the phone and dialled Peter Booth.

"Hi, Peter. It's Vikki. You were looking for me yesterday evening. Sorry I couldn't call you back. You caught me at a rather difficult moment, I'm afraid."

"Oh, sorry about that. I was just ringing to see when we might see each other again, that's all. How are you fixed this evening?"

"Not sure, yet. Sorry to be a pain. I'm not dodging you, honestly. It's just things are hotting up a bit here."

"Sounds interesting. Shall I call you later, then?" Booth said.

"Yes, thanks. Give me a ring when you're finishing up at work and we can see how the land lies. By the way, before you go, do you happen to know if Tiverton Transport use the other ports in the country like Dublin and Cork?"

"Not that again, Vikki. Haven't you had enough of Tiverton Transport to last you a lifetime after that disaster down here the other day?"

Kirkby noticed that Booth hadn't actually answered her question, but she didn't want to press him at this point.

"Yes, I guess you're right. Never mind. Talk later, OK?"

"Yes, I'll call you."

When she had finished the call, she had an idea. She telephoned her old station in Dublin and asked to be put through to Detective Sergeant Avril Cunningham. There were a few clicks, and then she recognised her former colleague's voice on the line.

"Wow, hello stranger," Cunningham said. "How the hell are you?"

Avril Cunningham had worked quite extensively with Kirkby when they were both stationed at Fitzgibbon Street Garda station in Dublin's city centre, and the two women had got on really well. Cunningham knew that Kirkby had been scapegoated before being posted to Wexford, and was pleased to hear from her old mate.

"Ah, ye know, Avril. Muddling along. But listen, I need a favour," Kirkby said. "Could you do a bit of discreet rooting around and see if a haulage firm called Tiverton Transport brings up any markers anywhere. I can't make it official just yet, but they have come up in connection with a case I'm working here in Wexford, and I'd be interested to know if there's anything on them in Dublin."

"OK, no problem. I'll have a snoop about."

Kirkby and Cunningham spent another fifteen minutes on the phone chatting about this and that. Kirkby told the Dublin-based detective that she was settling in reasonably well to her new situation, but she still missed the excitement of working in the capital.

"Don't worry, Vikki. If you manage to put this one to bed, they'll be screaming for you back here before long. I suppose you heard that DI Jameson is gone?"

"No, I didn't hear that. What's the story?"

"He's retired out on the sick. Stress, apparently. Serves him right if you ask me. They had no right to blame you for his cock-up," Cunningham said.

"God, that's gas. Did he decide to go himself or was he pushed?"

"We're not sure. There are rumours about both, but one thing is for certain, he's gone and he won't be back. I'd say someone further up the food chain knew exactly what he was up to and wouldn't have it. So, when the dust settles a bit, I'd say you'd be welcomed back with open arms here."

"Maybe I wouldn't want to come back. After all I'm a country girl at heart!" Kirkby said.

"OK. So, you've found a man then," Cunningham said, and the two women laughed out loud.

Chapter Twenty-Five

Noon came around all too quickly, and it seemed like only minutes since the three of them had been seated in Kirkby's office talking over the case.

"So, what have we got that's new?" Kirkby said, sipping coffee from a cardboard cup that Ciara Nestor had generously provided.

"I got back onto the DVLA, boss. Those plates that we found in Frank Roche's van belong to a number of scrapped cars in the UK. But forensics say they have been used at the back of trailers where the drivers attach them with rubber bands to a backing plate. There's residue on them all. And they are square too, which you don't get on many cars these days," Ciara Nestor reported.

"OK, thanks, Ciara. I'm afraid we're going to have to send you back to your spreadsheets. Can you see if the numbers match any of the records that Roche was keeping in his document vault?"

"Yes. That won't take long as I have the records all in Excel now," Nestor said.

"What about your investigations, Cathal? What have you got for us?" Kirkby said.

"Well, those ID plates you photographed on the trailers last night are bogus. The serial numbers are way out of range for Wexford. The guy said they won't be up to those numbers till well into the next century!"

"What about the Spaniard?" Kirkby said.

"I spoke to the Spanish police. They put me onto Tarragona. Apparently, Hernandez may have been active in that area recently. An Inspector Jefe – that's Chief Inspector – Gonzales is going to call me later," Waters said, smiling.

"Right, well stay on it, Cathal. This is important. OK. Let's see if we can piece this thing together a bit before I go upstairs. It looks to me like there's VAT fraud going on to do with the illegal importation of refrigerated three-axle trailers from the UK. Someone is bringing these things in fairly frequently, painting them up, and selling them on with false IDs as virtually new wagons. It could be worth a great deal of money, especially as we don't know as yet how extensive the business is. It could easily be in operation at the other ports in the country too, not just Rosslare," Kirkby said.

"So, Frank Roche finds out what is going on. He builds up a pile of evidence from the various customs clearance and waybill documents. But what does he do with that evidence that gets him killed, if that is why he was shot so brutally?" Nestor said.

"Follow the money, that's what I say," Waters said.

"Probably a very good idea, Cathal. What do we know about Roche's finances?" Kirkby said.

"Well, they had that nice little nest egg in the Credit Union," Waters said. "We don't know where exactly that

114

came from, though they could have saved it, I guess. It looks like the Roches lived very frugally."

"Why don't you get onto the Credit Union and see what you can find out, Cathal? And while you're at it, see what we can uncover about Danny Roche's finances. He drives a very new BMW that looks to me to be a bit above his pay grade. Did you get any information from the school about Eileen Roche's role?"

"Yes, I did. It all looks innocent enough. She was the bookkeeper at the school. Looked after all the money coming in and going out of the school's bank account – paying suppliers, staff, that sort of thing. The woman I spoke to says Eileen Roche was totally trustworthy. Salt of the earth, you know. But there was one rather odd thing. She wouldn't let me look in Mrs Roche's desk for some reason, which I thought was very peculiar," Waters said.

"You're right, that is odd. I wonder what she was trying to hide. Did she say if the school accounts were audited?" Kirkby said.

"Yes, she said they are. But she didn't say by whom."

"Hmm… get back onto her, and get the name of the auditors. They're bound to be a local firm. Then get onto them and see if they have anything to report that could be of interest."

"Can I say something, boss?" Ciara Nestor said.

"Yes, of course, Ciara. What is it?"

"Is this case going to be taken away from us?"

"Over my dead body, Ciara. No chance. If Frawley tries that on, you'll hear my screams all the way to the commissioner, and that's a promise!"

Ciara Nestor smiled.

* * *

Kirkby rang upstairs to make an appointment to see Superintendent Frawley early in the afternoon.

"He's out to lunch till about 2:30, Inspector, but I could slot you in then for fifteen minutes if that would suit?" the superintendent's assistant said.

"Yes, that would be fine. Thanks."

Kirkby decided she needed a decent lunch before facing down the superintendent, so she went outside to drive into town. It was still raining, but not as heavily as it had been, and the sky was a bit lighter. It looked as if it would be a fine afternoon when the clouds eventually moved away. Kirkby drove into the centre of Wexford, and parked close to the Talbot Hotel. She walked up King Street, as far as the intersection with South Main Street, and turning up along the busy thoroughfare, came to a tempting-looking café that was boasting all sorts of luncheon delights. Inside, Kirkby treated herself to homemade lasagne and chips. She wasn't going to face the afternoon on an empty stomach.

* * *

Frawley was in a surprisingly mellow mood when she entered his office at just on 2:30.

"Come in, Vikki. Take a seat. Can I get you a tea or a coffee?" Frawley said.

"No thanks, sir. I've just had lunch, but thank you all the same."

"Right. Well, tell me what you have got on the Roche case then," he said.

Kirkby outlined the progress that had been made since Frawley had set the deadline for her to relinquish the case. She explained about her visit to the yard where the smuggled trailers were being kept, leaving out any of the detail that he might construe as unorthodox. She also informed him about Ciara Nestor's findings on Tiverton Transport, and the false number plates that had been found in the back of Frank Roche's van.

"What about the Spanish connection – this man Fernandez or whatever his name is?"

"It's Hernandez, sir, and we have ongoing dialogue with the Spanish police. It seems he may be holed up in Tarragona. I'll know more later today," Kirkby said.

"I see. Well, it does seem like you are making some progress, however tenuous."

Kirkby spoke again before he could go on.

"I think it's a little better than that, sir. We now have a motive of sorts, and plenty more to follow up on. That's if you're happy to leave it with me, of course."

"Hmm... well, you know I'm going out on a bit of a limb for you here, Inspector. I've already had the press office on asking about the fiasco at the harbour, and I've only just managed to cover that little caper over. It would help if you could get some more concrete information on this trailer smuggling, and maybe make an arrest or two. Then we might be able to justify all that nonsense from the other day."

"I'd prefer to wait until our investigation has collected more evidence, sir. Everything we have now is a bit circumstantial. And if we go off half-cocked, we could lose the main prize, that being the Roches' killers."

"Very well. But don't let me down here, Inspector. There's a lot riding on this case, not just for you, but for all of us. And I want to be kept informed of progress every day for the next week at least. Now, why don't you go off and see if you can catch us some killers?"

And with that, the meeting was over. Kirkby didn't know exactly where she stood with Frawley, but she figured that he hadn't taken her off the case – not yet at least. But she recognised that she needed to bring this one home soon, and right now, she had no idea how that might be achieved.

Chapter Twenty-Six

When Kirkby got back downstairs, Cathal Waters followed her into her office.

"Can I have a word, boss?" he said.

"Yes, of course, Cathal, come in, take a seat."

Waters sat in the chair facing Kirkby's desk, but she noticed that he was upright and attentive, whereas before he would have been slouching untidily and a bit preoccupied.

"I've had a call back from Inspector Gonzalez from the police in Tarragona, boss. He says that they have had Hernandez in custody there for nearly a month. He was arrested during an armed raid on a wholesaler. Apparently, they were after the payroll. It seems that a lot of Spanish firms still pay their workers in cash."

"So, he was actually in their care when this all went down out at Tobinstown?"

"Yep, 'fraid so."

"Damn! How the hell did his dabs get on the cartridge we recovered from the shotgun then?" Kirkby said.

"It's a puzzle, isn't it. I suppose forensics could have got it wrong. Where does that leave us, boss?"

"In the proverbial, Cathal, that's where. Look, can you give Keith a call and ask him about the partial fingerprint. Get him to redo it and see if perhaps he wasn't mistaken originally. Did you find out anything about the school accounts yet?"

"I'm waiting on a call back from the auditors. They're a local firm, but the partner that handles the school wasn't available. I'll chase them up later if I haven't heard back."

"Great, thanks. Have you any idea how Ciara is getting on?"

"No, I haven't spoken to her. Will I ask her to come in?"

"Yes, please. Thanks."

A few moments later, Ciara Nestor appeared.

"Hi, Ciara. Come in. Have you made any progress?"

"Well, maybe. Sergeant Waters asked me to handle the Credit Union enquiry, as he was busy with the Spanish thing, and the other business with the school's auditors. I got to speak to a very helpful woman in the Credit Union. She told me that Eileen Roche was the one who did the regular withdrawals from their joint account. She always took it out in cash, usually near the end of the month."

"Did she happen to know what Mrs Roche was doing with the money?"

"Not exactly. But she quite often chatted to Mrs Roche. She said she was very friendly. She remembers her saying a couple of months back as Mrs Roche was collecting the money, 'That'll keep them going for another while.' The cashier didn't question the remark, but she thought it a bit odd."

"Hmm… strange, all right. Anything else?" Kirkby said.

"Not from the Credit Union. But I did the analysis you asked me to do on those registration plates. They don't seem to match any of the numbers from the trucks Roche had highlighted in his paperwork."

"Just our luck. Crikey, Ciara, we need a breakthrough in this bloody thing soon. Never mind Frawley, it's driving me mad as well. Anyway, thanks. I suppose you heard about the Spaniard?"

"No. What about him?"

"All nicely tucked up in a Spanish police cell at the time of the murders, so no joy there either."

* * *

As the afternoon wore on, Cathal Waters took a call from Kevin Armstrong from the firm of accountants that audited the school accounts.

"Good afternoon, Mr Armstrong. Thanks for calling me back. I just needed to have a word about the accounts for St Mary's school. I understand you are their auditors."

"Yes, that's right. It's a fairly straightforward job really. Never any issue there."

"That's good to hear. But may I ask if you ever spotted anything at all that puzzled you in the accounts? Anything that couldn't easily be justified or explained?"

"Hmm… let me think. Well, there was one thing that seemed a bit strange. But it was about money received, not expended, so I didn't pay it much heed," Armstrong said.

"Oh. What was that then?"

"Well, I don't suppose it's any secret, Sergeant, that the school was running on a shoestring. They were always short of money, even though they have a healthy facility at the bank. But that is nearly always used to the full, and the department aren't exactly generous. So, sometimes they have a bit of a struggle to meet the payroll. And that's the odd thing. On several occasions there appears to have been a deposit in the school's bank account of €1,000 just as the payroll came due. It has been enough to cover the shortfall every time, except at Christmas. But even then, the mysterious lodgement was increased by €1,500 to cover the bit extra that the staff get at that time of year."

"And did you ever find out where this money was coming from?"

"No. I asked Eileen Roche about it more than once, but she just said that it must be an anonymous benefactor. Things like that happen with schools sometimes, and as it wasn't money going out, we didn't bother too much about it. It's not all that unusual with institutions."

"I see. Was there anything else, Mr Armstrong?"

"No. Nothing more. If you're looking for a scandal to do with school accounts, Sergeant, you'll have to look elsewhere. St Mary's is squeaky clean."

"Well, thanks anyway, Mr Armstrong. I appreciate your candidness. Oh, just one final question. Where did the school hold its bank account?"

"That would be with the National Bank. The Redmond Square branch. They've had it there ever since I've been involved, and probably a lot longer."

"Thanks. That's very helpful."

"No problem. Always happy to help the police. Goodbye now."

When Waters had finished speaking to Mr Armstrong, he left the station and went to pay a call on the National Bank on Redmond Square before it closed at four o'clock.

Chapter Twenty-Seven

Kirkby needed cheering up. She dialled Peter Booth's number and was pleased when he answered sounding bright and breezy.

"Hello, Vikki, I was just thinking about you."

"Oh, that's nice, must be your sixth sense. Anyway, what are you up to?"

"Nothing much. We had a bit of a kerfuffle here earlier with one of the ferries. A lorry on board caught fire just as it was offloading. It was the fridge unit. We put it out fairly smartly, but it was a bit dramatic for a while. Anyway, how's you?"

"Fed up. Things are going badly. I need alcohol and some good company," Kirkby said.

"OK. Well, it will take me about half an hour to finish up here, but after that I'm all yours. Why don't you come out here and we can go on somewhere?"

"Sounds good. I'll see you in half an hour. Bye."

She felt better as soon as she had finished the call with Booth. She was definitely smitten, but she was enjoying it too. She wasn't sure to what extent he felt the same, and there hadn't been a chance to have anything like a serious talk with him about their feelings. But she hoped that the opportunity wouldn't elude them for much longer. She needed to know where she stood with men. Anything else made her uneasy.

* * *

Forty minutes later she pulled her car into the compound at Rosslare Harbour and parked. She got out, and stood for a few minutes enjoying the sea breeze and the view, which had improved greatly along with the weather since that morning. It wasn't long before she heard the door to the offices opening, and Booth coming across the car park in her direction with a big friendly smile on his face. He put his arms around her, and gave her a brief kiss on the lips, much to the delight of his co-workers who were looking out from the first-floor windows.

"Great to see you," he said, "where would you like to go?"

"Can we go for a walk, Peter? We can work up an appetite for later."

"Yes, OK. Let's take both cars and drive out to Carne," Booth said.

"Cool. I'll follow you."

They got into their respective vehicles and set off out of the harbour and onto the N25. When they got to Tagoat, they turned off towards Lady's Island and then on past the Lobster Pot down to the large car park at the front of the Carne Beach Caravan and Camping Park.

The incoming tide had softened what was left of the breeze, and when they walked through the dunes onto the beach itself, the sun was shining on the wide, golden sands. There was no one else to be seen on the beach at that time of day, although as they walked along holding hands, they passed the remains of sandcastles that had been created by children earlier.

They strolled along in companionable silence for a while, just enjoying the closeness and the scenery. Then Kirkby decided to broach the subject that had been on her mind.

"What's going to become of us, Peter?" she said.

"How do you mean?"

"I suppose I mean how serious are you about our relationship, that's all?"

"I very much enjoy being with you, Vikki. But beyond that I haven't really given it a whole lot of thought. Is that bad?" Booth said.

"No, of course not. But I have to confess, I'm getting a bit fond of you, you know. I was just wondering if you feel the same."

Booth stopped walking, faced Kirkby and drew her in for a long and passionate kiss. When he withdrew, he said, "Does that help to convince you?"

Kirkby snuggled in against his chest.

"A bit, I suppose. Look, I know I'm not in a position to make any demands of you. I just need to know where I stand, that's all."

"Let's just take it a day at a time for now. You know I have no other commitments, and no other close female friends. Let's just see how things go."

Kirkby said nothing. It wasn't what she wanted to hear, but it would have to do for the moment.

* * *

Later, as they were seated in the restaurant enjoying some really delicious food, Kirkby brought up another subject.

"By the way, I meant to ask. Does anyone down at the harbour check the number plates of the vehicles coming and going through the port?"

"Not specifically, unless we need to identify a particular unit for some reason or other."

"And if you do have to identify a particular lorry, do you check the front or the back plate?"

"Wow! What a question. What's this about?"

"Ah, possibly nothing. But humour me. Which do you check?" Kirkby said.

"Almost always the front number plate. Quite often some of the trailers don't even have a rear number plate. They fall off on the road and things, or maybe they even get nicked at the motorway services. They're usually just held on with rubber bands."

"So, you would use the numbers on the front of the tractor units for identification purposes."

"Yes, we would. Why?"

Kirkby thought for a moment before replying.

"I'm not sure if I should be telling you this, but we found a few square, yellow plates in the back of Frank Roche's van. We ran them against the DVLA in the UK, and they turned out to be false. We're just curious as to how he came by them, and what he was doing with them."

"Wow! That's definitely very strange. Have you found out what vehicles the plates belonged to?" Booth said.

"Just various cars that had been written off to scrap. But very few cars use square plates these days, so there's definitely something more to it. I'd say Frank Roche got them from the back end of trailers that came through the port, but as to why, I have no idea."

Chapter Twenty-Eight

The following morning, Peter Booth had left Kirkby's bed at 6:30. She was still asleep, so he just gave her a gentle kiss on the forehead before departing silently. She woke an hour later, surprised to find herself alone. She wondered why it was that Booth always left so early. She must ask him next time they got together.

As she was preparing for the day ahead, Kirkby had an idea. When she was showered and dressed, and had consumed a modest breakfast of cereal dotted with fresh blueberries, she called Cathal Waters on his mobile phone.

"Good morning, Cathal. It's me. Listen, I won't be in first thing this morning. I want to go back out to Tobinstown and have another look around. Sometimes, I find that going back to the scene helps to inspire some new angle. I'll see you at about eleven. OK?"

Waters was a bit puzzled by what he thought to be somewhat unusual behaviour, but he tried not to let it show.

"Yes, fine, boss. Do you want me to come out there too?"

"No, thanks, Cathal. You stay at the station and work with Ciara following up on the photos from the trailer repair place. Oh, there is one more thing too. Can you ask Ciara to get back onto the woman in the Credit Union? Get her to find out if they can remember how the lodgements to the Roches' account were made," Kirkby said.

"Right, will do. Talk to you later then."

* * *

It took Kirkby almost an hour to get from her home in Rosslare to the Roches' house. It was a nice bright sunny morning, so she decided to take the scenic route via Killinick, Mayglass, Tomhaggard and Grantstown, and on into Wellingtonbridge before joining the main R733 for the last part of the journey through Curraghmore and Ramsgrange. She pulled her car onto the grass verge outside the Roches' bungalow and got out.

The place seemed to her to be a bit more overgrown than the last time she had been there. She guessed that at this time of year, growth was at its peak, which accounted for the height of the grass and weeds surrounding the rather forlorn-looking dwelling. As she approached the gate onto the property, she spotted Michael Talbot marching down the road towards her with his dog on a lead. She waited until they were within speaking distance.

"Good morning," she said. "Mr Talbot, isn't it?"

"Yes, that's right. Apologies, I'm afraid you have the advantage over me."

"Sorry, I'm Detective Inspector Vikki Kirkby. We met the day Mr and Mrs Roche were found."

"Yes, of course. I'm sorry. Have you managed to catch anyone yet? The whole neighbourhood is still feeling very nervous after those terrible events."

"We are following some definite lines of enquiry, Mr Talbot. I was wondering if you have remembered anything further from the time it happened? I think you said you had seen the couple when you were out for a walk."

"Yes, that's right, although it was the Roches that were out walking. I was in my garden, but no, I can't say I have remembered anything else."

"And you're certain you didn't see anyone else around that evening at all."

"No, no one. Apart from their son, Danny, of course. Well, I didn't actually see him, just his car. It was parked in about the same place as yours is now, but there was nothing unusual about that. He was quite a frequent visitor," Talbot said.

"Did you tell any of the Gardaí about seeing Danny's car?"

"I can't really remember, Inspector. The whole thing is a bit of a blur to be honest. I may have done. Why? How could that be significant?"

"It probably isn't, Mr Talbot. It's just a detail that we may have overlooked. You never know what's important in these situations. And you are sure it was Danny's car you saw?"

"Yes, well I'm almost certain. We don't get too many of those smart BMWs around here."

"I don't suppose you remember any of the registration number, or anything?"

"No, of course not. I'm not very observant in that regard, Inspector, but I'm almost sure it was his car. "

"OK. Well thanks for the information in any case, Mr Talbot. If we need anything more, we'll be in touch."

Michael Talbot continued his walk back along the narrow road and up around the corner towards his own house, till he was out of sight.

Kirkby mooched around the old house for a few more minutes. She didn't go in, and as nothing new presented itself, other than the revelation from Michael Talbot, she got back into her car and made a phone call.

"Hi, Peter, it's me," she said when she got through to Peter Booth.

"Oh, hi. Sorry, it's a bit busy here just now. Can I call you back?"

"This won't take a sec. I just need to find out if Tiverton Transport have regular comings and goings in Cork. Who should I speak to down there?"

"Christ, Vikki, I wish you'd leave this Tiverton thing alone. Haven't you established that they are just a legitimate transport company? If you harass them any further, they'll put in a complaint about you."

Kirkby was taken aback by Booth's defence of the company. What she was doing was no skin off his nose, unless of course he was involved in some way. She had an uneasy feeling creeping over her.

"OK. Never mind. I'll find out for myself. I just thought you might have a contact in the port down there, that's all. Sorry to have bothered you."

She hung up before he could reply. The next call she made was to Ciara Nestor.

"Hi, Ciara, it's me. Look, I need you to do something for me. Can you find out which Garda station in Cork has oversight of the port. And then give them a call and find out who we can talk to in the harbour that could give us information about traffic movements. I'll be back in about an hour. Is everything else OK?"

"Yes, boss. I'll get onto it straight away. See you in a while."

"Yes, thanks, Ciara. Bye."

* * *

Cathal Waters called the Credit Union and got speaking to the woman they had previously dealt with over the Roches' account. When he had introduced himself, he said, "Sorry to trouble you again, Margaret, but I was wondering if you can remember anything about the lodgements to the Roches' account."

"How do you mean?"

"Well, can you recall if the lodgements were in cash or by cheque?"

"Gosh, we get such a lot of transactions through here, it's hard to remember. Hold on a second and I'll just ask Fintan if he remembers anything. He dealt with the Roches sometimes too."

Waters could hear the mumbled sounds of Margaret talking to her colleague with her hand over the mouthpiece of the telephone. After a few sentences had been exchanged, she was back on the line.

"I've spoken to Fintan, officer, and I remember now. Some of the lodgements were in cash, but sometimes Mr Roche gave us a sterling cheque. That was quite awkward for us, because, you know, we don't do our own clearing, so we had to send it down the road and wait for the bank to clear it and give us credit. But Mr Roche was a patient man, and he was always very understanding."

"I see. I don't suppose you recall any details about the cheques he gave you?" Waters said.

"No, I don't," Margaret said, audibly rather put out that the detective expected her to, "but with those things we always have to take a copy of the item before we send it to the bank in case it gets lost, or something."

"So, you have photocopies of the cheques then?" Waters said, his interest piqued.

"Well, yes. But it's a while since, so it would take me a little while to locate them. Our filing system here is a bit basic."

Waters detected that the woman was smiling slightly, probably from embarrassment.

"Well, Margaret, I wonder if you could manage to find them for me? Sometime over the next few days would be fine. Maybe you could let me know when you have them, and I'll stop by and collect the details?"

"Yes, yes, I suppose so. I'll see if I can get to it tomorrow and I'll call you. Is that OK?"

"Perfect. Thanks very much, Margaret."

Chapter Twenty-Nine

Kirkby was back at the Garda headquarters in Wexford by just after eleven o'clock. She brewed a coffee, and then asked Waters and Nestor to join her in her office.

"Right, guys, we have some new information. It turns out Daniel Roche was probably at his parents' house on the evening they were killed. The neighbour, Talbot, now remembers that he saw Danny's car outside the place, which means that Danny may have lied to us. Talbot didn't remember the number plate, but he said he was almost certain it was Danny's BMW. So, I'd like us to concentrate on Danny Roche for the rest of the day. Ciara, did you get any information from Cork about who runs the harbour facility down there?"

"Yes, boss. There's a man called Séamus Cullinane who seems to be the bloke in charge."

"Great, thanks, Ciara. Did Cork want to know why you were interested?"

"No, they didn't seem too bothered," Nestor said.

"Good. Let's deal with it on a need-to-know basis only, for now."

"OK, boss."

"And I have something to report as well," Waters said.

"Sorry, Cathal. What have you got?"

Waters told them what he had discovered speaking to Margaret at the Credit Union.

"That's good work, Cathal. Let me know as soon as she gets back to you with the information from the sterling cheques. I'd better go and have a word upstairs and see if we can get in front of Danny Roche without causing a major diplomatic incident," Kirkby said.

"It might be best if we got Cork to lift him and bring him here, boss. What do you think?" Waters said.

"It probably would be, Cathal, but it's not my style. I want to catch him unawares before he has hours to make up some kind of a story. And we might be able to kill two birds with one stone, if we're lucky. So not a word to anyone, but be prepared for a bit of a drive in an hour or so."

"Hmm... OK, boss."

* * *

Superintendent Liam Frawley was in his office when Vikki Kirkby knocked on the door.

"Come in, Vikki. How are things?" he said.

Kirkby entered the office and took a seat in front of the man who was seated behind his expansive desk.

"Progressing nicely, at last, sir." She brought him up to date with the latest information that she had in relation to the double murder.

"So, sir, I want to go to Cork to interview Danny Roche, but I don't want him to know we are coming. I was wondering if you could square it for me with the Cork Gardaí? I can't afford to upset anyone down there."

Frawley grunted, as if he was processing what more disruption this woman could bring to the case.

"Is that absolutely necessary, Inspector? Can you not just get the Cork lads to bring him here? It would be much simpler."

"Well, sir, with respect, I don't want him to have time to make up a story. I want to confront him when he's not expecting it, otherwise he'll put together some yarn. We know he's lied to us already about the last time he saw his parents," Kirkby said.

"Seems a bit over top to me, Inspector."

"Well, sir, there is more."

"Oh? What's that then?"

"Danny Roche seems to be living well above his means, sir. I think he may be involved in something dodgy," Kirkby said. She knew she was stretching the facts a little to suit her own agenda, but she was determined to have her way.

"Oh, very well then. I'll give Chris Mulvaney a call and tell him what you're up to. He'll square it with Anglesea Street. But for Christ's sake, try not to cause a rumpus. That's all we bloody need."

"Thank you, sir. I'd better get going and make the arrangements."

"Right. Keep me informed please."

"Of course, sir, and thank you."

Kirkby got up and left the superintendent in rather a grumpy mood, but at least she had got what she wanted.

* * *

Back downstairs she summoned Cathal Waters into her office.

"Come in, Cathal. How do you fancy a trip to Cork?"

"Danny Roche?"

"Exactly." Kirkby was impressed that her sergeant made the connection so quickly. He was coming on.

"Can you get Ciara to make a call to the harbour company down there and ask to speak to him on some pretext. She can just hang up if she gets through, or whatever. I want to make sure he's actually working today before we schlep all the way down there. How long does it take to get to Cork anyway?"

"About two and a half hours or thereabouts, depending on the traffic," Waters said.

"Perfect. Go and ask Ciara to make the call, and then we'll leave in half an hour. That'll get us there just as he's finishing his day's work."

"Righto, boss." He left the room in search of his colleague.

* * *

Half an hour later, Kirkby and Waters were in Kirkby's car leaving Wexford. Ciara Nestor had confirmed that Danny Roche was at work, so they assumed he would be finishing sometime between five and six o'clock. Waters had brought a bag containing a couple of sandwiches for them to consume en route, and some fizzy drinks to accompany the food. The weather was warm, but overcast as they set off. Kirkby decided to follow the N25 for the entire route that would take them via New Ross, Waterford, Dungarvan and Midleton. They wouldn't have to wrestle with the Cork traffic, as the harbour had moved downstream some years ago and was now conveniently positioned on the east side of the city close to Little Island.

"So, Cathal, how do you think we're getting on?" Kirkby asked as they left Wexford behind them and the road opened up.

"How do you mean, boss?"

"Well, are you happy working with me? Do you think we make a good team?"

"I guess we're OK. I've never worked for a female DI before, but so far, so good. What do you think?"

"I think it's going quite well. You have improved measurably since I arrived, and I have a feeling you could probably go a bit further too. What are your ambitions, Cathal?"

"I haven't thought about it much, to be honest. I'm quite happy as a detective sergeant, boss."

"I think you should set your sights a bit higher. If we manage to crack this case, I'll make sure you get a good mention upstairs. You should be thinking about getting inspector in a year or two. Have you strong ties to Wexford?"

"Not really. My folks are from the town, but we're not terribly close. I have a brother and a sister, but they both left Wexford a few years back. My sister is in London working for a television production company, and my brother is in Dublin teaching. It wouldn't bother me if I was transferred to another town in the south here, though preferably not Cork," Waters said.

"Why not Cork?"

"Ah, ye know. Some of them have fierce ideas about themselves. I don't think I'd fit in. But Waterford or Dungarvan would be fine if it came to it, or even Youghal at a push."

"That's a good attitude to have. I'm going to pull in soon and we can eat our lunch. Do you mind if we stop at a petrol station and get some hot drinks to go with the sandwiches? I don't want to fill myself up with gassy drinks," Kirkby said.

"No, that's fine. Good idea."

They settled into quiet harmony for the next few miles.

Chapter Thirty

It was coming up to five o'clock when Vikki Kirkby pulled her car into the expansive car park of the Port of Cork Company's offices. The port authority had been named thus in 1997, modernising the old nineteenth-century title of the Cork Harbour Commissioners. Kirkby looked around at the twenty or so cars parked around the perimeter and saw a smart-looking black BMW tucked in between a Ford Mondeo and a silver VW Caddy van.

"Is that chummy's Beemer over there," she said, nodding in the direction of the car.

Waters consulted his notebook. "Yep, that's it. What do we do now?"

"Nothing. We sit here till he comes out and then we have a little chat with him."

"Do you want to bring him in to Anglesea Street?" Waters said.

"Not unless he starts acting silly buggers. I just need to find out why he lied to us about being at his parents' house that night, that is assuming Michael Talbot got it right."

"Do you think he was involved in their deaths?" Waters said.

"I've no idea, Cathal. That's what we need to find out."

The two of them sat in silence for several minutes, before the doors to the offices opened, and three people came out, talking amongst themselves. Danny Roche was one of the trio. The three chatted away for a few minutes, and then they said goodbye, with Danny waving briefly to the others. He set off towards his car.

"Right, let's go," Kirkby said, opening the door of her car and stepping out onto the concrete yard.

Waters followed suit, and they walked towards Danny Roche's car, which was some thirty metres away. Danny Roche saw the two detectives advancing towards him and panicked. He ran to the car, blipping the key fob so that the car doors unlocked before he got to it. He jumped in, and deftly started the car, spinning the wheels as he gunned the motor, taking off across the car park.

"Shit!" Kirkby barked. "Quick, back to the car."

Kirkby and Waters got back into their car as quickly as they could. Kirkby started the engine and set off as quickly as she dared in pursuit of the BMW. But her vehicle was no match for the powerful machine, and all she could do was watch hopelessly as the fleeing young man disappeared around a bend some way in front of the detectives. Kirkby drove as quickly as she could after the vanishing suspect, but by the time she got to the roundabout where the exit road from the harbour joined several other roads, her quarry had simply vanished.

"Shit, shit, shit!" she said again. "What the hell do we do now?" It what more or less a rhetorical question, because she knew full well what had to be done. She pulled the car over, parking on the hard shoulder with her hazard lights flashing.

Kirkby called Anglesea Street Garda station, and asked for Inspector Chris Mulvaney. After a few clicks and rather too much inane music, she finally got through to the man. She introduced herself and explained the situation.

"I see," Mulvaney said surprisingly calmly. "And what would you like us to do now, then, Inspector?"

"I need to find Danny Roche. Could I ask you to circulate his details and issue a stop-and-detain order for me? My sergeant has the car registration here, and we can give you a description as well."

"Hmm… can I ask what exactly Mr Roche has done, Inspector?" Mulvaney said.

"We need to speak to him in connection with a double murder at Tobinstown, near Wexford."

"All right. I can put out the message, but if we do find him, we won't be able to hold him for long, so we'll need to have you available if you intend to question him or arrest him."

"Yes, that's not a problem. I'll stay around for the rest of the evening here in Cork, and even if I'm back in Wexford, that's only a couple of hours away. Can I hand you over to Sergeant Waters to copy down the rest of the information?" Kirkby said.

"Yes, very well."

Waters took Kirkby's phone and recited the details of Danny Roche's car; a description of the man; the address that they had for him in Cork; and Kirkby's phone number, adding his own for good measure.

When the call was ended, Waters said to Kirkby, "Where to now, boss?"

"I know it's a long shot, Cathal, but let's head over to Danny's address and see if by any chance he's turned up there."

"It's hardly likely, is it, boss?"

"Maybe not, but have you got any better ideas?"

Waters just grunted.

* * *

Danny Roche's address was a gated estate of just twenty-five houses in the upmarket area of Montenotte. The estate was shaped like a horseshoe with the houses surrounding a large open grassed area that was well maintained. Some small trees had been planted around the perimeter, and a few children's toys lay scattered about. Number twelve was along the left-hand flank of the estate. It was a modern, spacious, detached property with a decent-sized front garden, and a tidy tarmac driveway. There was no sign of the car, nor any other indication that there was anyone home.

Kirkby pulled the car up outside and Waters and herself got out.

"You go around the back, just in case, Cathal. I'll ring the doorbell," Kirkby said.

"Right boss."

Kirkby approached the front of the house and stepped up to the door. She rang the bell, and stood back and to the side by way of self-protection. But there was no reply. She rang again, this time more persistently, but still there was no response. As she turned away, Waters came back around.

"No sign of anyone out back, boss. Have you had any luck?"

"No. Nothing."

The two detectives started walking back down the drive towards their car, when they heard a voice calling them.

"Hello. Hello. Can I help you?"

The voice belonged to a tall, rather portly man who was emerging from the house next door. He was dressed in a pair of khaki-coloured slacks and a green V-necked pullover, and was well-groomed with tightly trimmed grey hair. Kirkby judged the man to be in his sixties, or thereabouts.

"Hello. We were looking for Danny Roche," Waters said.

"Oh. You just missed him. He was here a few minutes ago. He drove up in a big hurry, dashed into the house, and came out after a couple of minutes with a black bag and took off at high speed. May I ask who you are?"

"I don't suppose he said where he was going?" Kirkby said.

"No. I didn't actually speak to him. I was in the front room just looking out the window," the man said.

"Oh, OK. Well, thanks anyway," Kirkby said turning away and walking back to the car. They both got in and Kirkby set off again.

"What now, boss?" Waters said.

Kirkby was getting fed up with Waters' apparent lack of initiative. She felt that she was constantly dragging him along, and the events of the day hadn't helped, although she had to admit, none of it was his fault.

"What do you suggest, Cathal?"

Waters thought for a moment.

"Why don't we go back to the Silver Springs hotel and get something to eat. We can wait for the lads from Cork to nab your man, and then be ready to spring back into action."

"OK. Sounds like a plan. I could do with some food anyway."

Chapter Thirty-One

The Silver Springs provided the two detectives from Wexford with sumptuous fare. It wasn't cheap, but it was very good, and when they had eaten their fill, they sat back in the lounge, nursing coffees. Waters had wanted a pint of Guinness, but Kirkby managed to persuade him to desist, given that they might be called into action at any moment.

But as the evening wore on, their hopes began to fade, and by 9:30 Kirkby was getting very fed up just hanging around.

"This is hopeless, Cathal. We might as well drive back to Wexford for all the good we are doing here. I'll keep my phone on overnight in case anything breaks. Can you do the same?"

"Yes, OK, boss."

They were nearly an hour into their journey, just approaching Dungarvan, when Kirkby's phone rang. It was connected to the hands-free Bluetooth system in her car, so the caller's name popped up on the screen in the centre of the dashboard. It was Peter Booth.

Kirkby pressed a button on the steering wheel, and the call was answered.

"Hi, babe," Booth said, "how's it going?"

"This isn't a very good time, Peter. Could I call you back?"

"Aw, shucks. And there was I hoping for a nice cosy evening with you in front of your TV, even if it was switched off!" Booth said.

Waters looked at Kirkby, somewhat bemused.

"I'm driving, Peter, and I have Sergeant Waters with me. Look, I'll call you back later on. Bye." She pressed another button on the steering wheel cutting off her somewhat overeager suitor.

"Is that Peter Booth who works out at Rosslare Harbour, boss?"

"Yes. The very same. Why?"

"Are you going out with him, boss?"

"What's it to you?"

Waters said nothing for a few moments, and then continued rather hesitantly.

"I suppose you know he's got form."

"How do you mean?"

"He got a suspended sentence around two years ago for assaulting a traffic warden in the town. And he had to pay a couple of thousand in compo to the woman."

"Are you serious? What happened?"

"He was given a ticket for parking on double yellows on the Crescent. When he got back to the car, the traffic warden that had ticketed him was nearby, so he got into a row and clocked her one. He knocked her to the ground and she was quite badly bruised. He called her some choice names too. Apparently, he made a right spectacle of himself. There was no shortage of witnesses. The council insisted on prosecuting him to demonstrate that they wouldn't tolerate that kind of thing. It was in the local paper and everything. I take it you didn't know?"

"Eh... no, I didn't. Is there anything else I should know about Mr Booth?"

"Not that I am aware of. Has he given you a smack yet?" Waters said, grinning.

"Feck off, Cathal. Do you think I'd stand for any of that crap? No, he certainly hasn't, and he isn't going to either."

Waters said nothing. He just sat back and smirked, looking out of the passenger window so that she couldn't see his face.

* * *

It was close to midnight when Kirkby finally got home to her house at Rosslare Strand. She had dropped Waters off at the station in Wexford to collect his car, and then driven on back herself. She was feeling very down in the dumps.

When she got indoors, she made herself a hot chocolate, and sat on the sofa contemplating her situation. Tomorrow, she would have to face the wrath of Superintendent Frawley, who would no doubt be livid at her incompetence. Heaven knows what he might do, but she was sure it wouldn't be good in any case. Then there was the issue with her new boyfriend. If Booth was a bit handy with his fists, she wanted nothing more to do with him. Men who hit women were a complete no-no in her books. She had seen enough broken and battered bodies of victims when she was working in Dublin, and pathetic men who kept saying, "I love her. I promise I won't do it again." But they always did, and for some reason the women mostly hung around. But not Vikki Kirkby.

When she had finished ruminating about those two problems, the spectre of the banter that would undoubtedly be circulating in the Garda station the next day came into her head. "Damn, I should have stayed in Dublin and taken the medicine," she said to herself as she trooped sluggishly up to bed feeling very sorry for herself. She brushed her teeth, got undressed and fell into bed, but sleep eluded her. She tried reading, but she could barely focus on her Kindle. She listened to the radio which was playing gentle, soporific tunes at that time of night, but that didn't do it either.

By 2:30, wide awake, she sat up in bed, and decided she would have to make a plan, and it would have to be a good one at that. She took a notebook and pen and constructed three scenarios that might get her out of the worst of the flak and restore some credibility to her reputation as a detective. One, in particular, would take her further out on a limb as far as procedure was concerned, but she calculated that it had the best chance of success. Somewhat relieved, she closed the book and lay back in the bed. She was asleep two minutes later.

At 5:45 a.m., the phone on Kirkby's nightstand started to jangle. It took a few moments to wake her from a deep sleep, but then she reached out and looked at the screen before answering. She didn't recognise the number, and hoped it wasn't someone from Asia trying to relieve her of her meagre savings with a scam call.

"Kirkby," she said on answering.

"Ah, Inspector. It's Sergeant Casey here from Anglesea Street in Cork. I'm the night man here at the station, and we have someone here who you might be interested in."

"Good morning, Sergeant. And who might that be?"

"One Daniel Roche, he says."

"Excellent. Where did you find him?" Kirkby said.

"Well, that's the funny thing. We got him down at Little Island in the back of the cab of a lorry waiting to board the ferry. He was all trussed up like a turkey with duct tape everywhere and a black plastic sack wrapped tightly around his middle."

"Wow! And how exactly did you find him?"

"Ah, now, when the driver went into the hut to see to his documents, yer man managed to get a leg free and rested his foot on the truck's horn. One of the customs men went to investigate and found him. He's been bashed around a bit, but he's mostly in one piece."

"I see. I don't suppose you know who owned the truck?"

"Oh, I do indeed. It's some crowd called Tiverton Transport. It's been seized in any case. It won't be going anywhere for a while, and we have the driver here too."

"Good stuff. Where is Roche now?"

"He's with me, but one of the lads is going to take him over to the hospital to have him checked out. He's blabbering like a spoilt child too. He seems to think he was going to be dumped overboard. So, we thought you should know," Casey said.

"Yes, thanks very much, Sergeant. I'll get back to you in a while. I have to make some arrangements," Kirkby said.

"Fair enough. Goodnight, ma'am."

Kirkby could tell that Sergeant Casey had a broad grin on his face as he bade her goodbye.

She was wide awake now, but it was too early to start calling people, and in any case, she wasn't quite sure what was best to do. This wasn't any part of any of her three plans, so she needed to do some more thinking. But she was glad that Danny Roche hadn't ended up feeding the fishes off the south coast of Ireland.

Chapter Thirty-Two

When the clock rolled around to 8 a.m., Kirkby felt that she could start calling people. Her first call was to Cathal Waters, who, surprisingly, seemed to be wide awake and fully alert. She filled him in on the news she had from Cork.

"What do you want to do, boss?"

"I need to talk to Frawley. I want him to work his magic with the Cork lads to make sure we can move

Roche and the lorry driver up here. I'd like you to get on the road. Bring a van and a uniformed Garda with you too. But don't arrive at Anglesea Street till you hear from me. OK?"

"Yes, OK. But what if Frawley doesn't go along with you? We will have wasted a whole day just driving around the countryside in a draughty van," Waters said.

"Trust me, Cathal. It will be fine."

By 8:30 Kirkby was showered and had downed a hasty slice of toast. She decided it wasn't too early to call Superintendent Frawley, so she dialled his mobile number.

Frawley recognised her number as he answered the call. "Yes, Inspector. What's up? I'm just trying to have my breakfast here," he said, rather tersely.

"Sorry to disturb you, sir, but I just thought you should know that Cork have Danny Roche in custody." She went on to relate the story that Sergeant Casey had told her about Roche's adventures down at Cork port.

"I was wondering if you could square it with your colleague in Cork for us to collect Roche and the driver, and bring them here, sir?"

Frawley said nothing for a minute, and Kirkby thought she could detect chewing noises over the phone.

"And what exactly are you planning on charging them with, Inspector?"

"Well, Roche ran off at high speed when we arrived down there to question him. He has lied to us about being at his parents' house the night they were killed, and from what I can see he's living well beyond his means, so there may be a lot more for him to talk to us about too. And there's definitely a connection to this Tiverton outfit as well."

"Ah, Tiverton be damned. If there's something going on there you need to hand that over to the right people. I'm only concerned with the killings."

Kirkby recognised the tactic. It was just a diversion while Frawley processed what the consequences might be for himself if he got stuck in and everything went pear-shaped.

"The first step would be to grill Danny Roche, sir, and I'd rather do it here than in Cork."

She had the good sense to say nothing more. She knew that the next person to speak would have lost the argument. A stony silence ensued, but just before it became embarrassing, Frawley said, "Very well. I'll give Chris Mulvaney a call for you. But hear this, Inspector. If this goes wrong, and you have put me in an awkward spot, you'll be back in uniform writing parking tickets for the rest of your career in the Gardaí. Do you understand?"

"Yes, sir. Of course. Thank you."

Kirkby ended the call. She wasn't quite sure how she felt about it all. She was convinced that Danny Roche was up to his neck in whatever was going on, but she was distinctly lacking any hard evidence. This wasn't going to be easy, at least not if she played by the book. She quickly got her stuff together and left the house to drive into Wexford.

* * *

It was mid-afternoon by the time Cathal Waters arrived back in Wexford with Danny Roche and the driver of the truck in which he had been found. Waters had had to go to the hospital to collect Roche. They had kept him in for a few hours for observation, but apart from some very obvious bruising about his person, there appeared to be little or no permanent damage.

Waters booked the two suspects in with the desk sergeant who showed them to two separate cells, removing any of their clothing that might be used for self-harm. The two men were sullen and dejected, and said almost nothing.

Waters then went to find Kirkby who was seated alongside Ciara Nestor in the open-plan, studying spreadsheets on a PC.

"I have the two boyos from Cork downstairs, boss. How do you want to play it?"

"Let's give them half an hour or so to settle into their new surroundings, and then we can go and have a chat. I want all three of us involved," Kirkby said.

"Frawley only allows two of us in with a suspect at a time, boss. Apparently, it's some new rule to do with human rights," Waters said.

"That's OK. You and I can start with Danny, and then depending on what he says, two of us will go and tackle the driver. What's his name, by the way?"

"He calls himself Earl Defoe. He's, eh, well you know."

"No, Cathal I don't know. What is he?"

"He's black, boss."

"Oh, right. Well, that doesn't make any difference. Not to me anyway. Did Cork check out his credentials?"

"Oh, yes. He's English, and his driver's license and tachograph were all in order. He apparently works for an agency. He's not employed by Tiverton."

"Right, well let's save all that till later. We'll go down soon and get started. OK?"

"Yes, boss," Waters and Nestor said in unison.

* * *

Danny Roche looked a little pathetic sitting in the interview room when Kirkby and Waters entered. The newly acquired decorations to his somewhat baby-like face didn't improve his appearance, and he was also very subdued and clearly quite nervous.

"Well, Danny. You certainly know how to live the high life," Kirkby said when she had completed all the usual formalities. "Care to tell us about it?"

Roche went on the defensive immediately.

"Why have you brought me here? What am I supposed to have done?"

Kirkby looked at her colleague.

"For starters, you ran off when we approached you outside your office in Cork, and drove off recklessly and at high speed," Waters said.

"So, give me a speeding ticket and let me out of here then," Roche replied sullenly.

"It's not quite that simple, I'm afraid, Danny. You see we have information from a witness that says that you lied to us about the last time you saw your parents. And lying to the police is never a good idea. And anyway, it looks as if we saved your life, so perhaps a little gratitude wouldn't go amiss. But what I really want to know is how exactly you are involved with Tiverton Transport and their vehicles?" Kirkby said.

"I don't know what you're talking about," Roche replied.

"I see. So how do account for the fact that you were discovered tied up in the cab of one of their lorries about to board the ferry?" she went on.

"Dunno. It must have been a case of mistaken identity. I haven't done anything."

"I don't believe you, Danny. I think you're up to your neck in it, and I intend to find out, whether you tell me or not. How much do you earn in your job, Danny?" Kirkby asked.

"None of your business."

"OK. We will find out from Revenue in any case, but I doubt if it's enough to sustain the lifestyle you're used to. That's a very big house you have in Montenotte, not to mention your nice new car."

Roche said nothing, but looked down at the floor.

"So, who disliked you enough to want to feed you to the fishes in the Irish Sea, Danny, and why?"

"I told you. Mistaken identity."

Kirkby tapped Cathal Waters with her foot underneath the table, out of sight of Danny Roche.

Waters leaned forward. "Tell us about the night your parents were shot, Danny."

"What about it?"

"We have a witness who places you outside their house at roughly the time the crime was committed, yet you told us that you hadn't seen them for two weeks before they were killed," Waters said.

"I got confused. I was in shock when I heard what had happened. I did visit them that night. But when I left, they were fine. Just watching telly beside the fire."

"And what time did you leave them, Danny?" Waters went on.

"I can't be sure, but I remember it was getting dark, so probably about ten o'clock. I had work the following day, so I didn't want to be too late."

Waters looked at Kirkby who nodded imperceptibly.

"That's interesting, Danny, because the pathologist tells us that your parents were killed before ten o'clock. Tell me, Danny, have you ever used a twelve-bore shotgun?" Waters said, stretching the pathologist's evidence just a little.

"No, of course not. And your pathologist is wrong. As I said, my parents were alive and well when I left them. Why would I want to kill my own parents anyway? That's disgusting."

Waters looked at Kirkby again, and she took over the interview.

"Tell us what you know about Tiverton Transport, Danny."

"Nothing. I've never heard of them."

"Really. Yet there you were all packaged up nicely in one of their trucks just waiting to board the ferry to England as their guest, and you say you've never heard of them. I thought you worked in Customs and Excise."

"I do. But that doesn't mean that we know all the hauliers by name. I've probably seen them coming and going through the port, but you get so as you don't take any notice after a while."

"So, you have no connection with that company at all, then. Is that right?"

"Yes. Correct."

"Tell me, Danny, what do you know of your parents' finances?"

"Nothing. Why would I? That was their business. I never borrowed any money from them. They didn't have anything to spare anyway."

"So, it would surprise you to find that your parents had nearly €50,000 in a Credit Union account in Wexford then?" Kirkby said.

"That's rubbish. Where would they get that kind of money?"

"Where, indeed!" Kirkby said.

"Now when are you going to let me out of here? I haven't done anything, and I'm sore as hell after that business with the lorry."

"Not so fast, Danny. We haven't finished with you yet. I need to consult with a colleague to see if we can charge you with obstruction. You may as well relax, you'll be here for a while yet."

Kirkby nudged Waters and they both got up and left the room. When they were back upstairs, they went into Kirkby's office.

"Well. What do you think, Cathal?"

"He's a cool customer, that's for sure. But as long as he sticks to that story, we haven't really got anything on him. Talbot's sighting of his car is bugger all use. He didn't see Danny in person, so it would never stand up. And a charge of obstruction probably wouldn't stick either, boss."

"Yes, I know. I just said that to manage his expectations of getting out soon."

"So, what do you want to do?"

"Leave him where he is while we go and talk to the driver. Then we'll have to bail him pending further enquiries," Kirkby said.

"Do you fancy him for the murders?"

"No, actually I don't. But he's heavily involved in this whole thing in some way or another, and I mean to find out how."

* * *

When Kirkby and Waters entered the interview room, Earl Defoe was sitting impatiently tapping his feet on the floor. He probably knew he could be in some serious trouble, but he probably reckoned they were just some sleepy out-of-town cops that he could blag pretty easily and get himself away unscathed.

Kirkby advised him of his rights, and the right to have a lawyer present, to which he replied, "What exactly are you charging me with, officer?"

Kirkby sat back in her chair before replying.

"Let's see, Earl. Kidnap just about fits the bill, wouldn't you say so? Then we'll add GBH in for good measure. You'll probably get a few years banged up here in Ireland, so I hope the folks back home won't miss you too much."

"I ain't done nothing. That geezer just showed up in my wagon when I was inside doing the paperwork. I don't know how he got there."

Kirkby looked at Waters and they both laughed.

"Yeah, right," she said. "Tell us another one, Earl. Very good."

"It's true. I never seen him before, and to be honest, I didn't even know he was there till all the bizzies started swarming around the wagon with the noise the damn thing was making."

"OK. But you should know that we recovered the bindings and the plastic that Mr Roche was restrained in, and we're having them forensically examined right now. A dollar gets you ten we find your big ugly paw prints all over the stuff," Waters said.

"I know what this is," Defoe said, "it's racist shit, innit? You lot think just cos I'm a bruvver, you can fit me up for anything you like."

"But, Earl, we don't need to fit you up. You're banged to rights as it is," Kirkby said.

Just then, there was a knock at the door and a uniformed Garda entered the room. He beckoned to Kirkby, and when she was standing close to him, he whispered, "Nothing, Inspector. No dabs anywhere. Nothing to tie this guy to Danny Roche. Sorry."

"Shit!" she replied. "OK. Thanks anyway."

Kirkby signalled to Waters that they should leave the room.

When Earl Defoe saw that they were off, he said, "Hey, where are you going? I need to get out of here."

Kirkby said nothing. The two detectives just left him to his thoughts.

Chapter Thirty-Three

The detectives reconvened upstairs in the open-plan. Vikki Kirkby was the first to speak.

"Well, guys, what do you think? Have we enough to charge either of them with anything substantial, or perhaps more importantly can we tie Danny to the murder of his parents?"

"I don't think we have anything, boss," Waters proposed. "We might get an obstruction charge to stick on Danny, but a decent brief would rip it apart. He'd play the distressed and bereaved son and all that, and we wouldn't stand a chance with the DPP."

"Terrific. What about Defoe?"

"Same. After all, what did he do?" Waters said.

"Shit, shit, shit! So, what the bloody hell do we do now then?"

Ciara Nestor put up her hand a little tenuously.

"Yes, Ciara?" Kirkby said.

"Why don't we release the pair of them on bail pending further enquiries, but follow them at a discreet distance. They are bound to be a bit rattled by today, and they might just lead us to whoever is behind this."

"Hmm… I see what you mean. But we'd need to be very careful. This lot aren't idiots. Listen, if we let them go, they have no transport up here, and Danny at least will want to get back to Cork. He'll have to return to work pretty smartish, and the other guy will want to get his lorry away on the ferry. Neither of them has met you, Ciara. It might be best if you follow them when we release them and see what they get up to. Would you be up for that?"

Nestor looked at the other two. "Yeah, I guess. Would I be on my own?"

"No, of course not. We'd be behind you, but at a distance. Are you up for it?"

"Yes, OK. I'll get a radio set so I can keep in touch with you both. Give me fifteen minutes to get organised and move my car outside the compound."

"Great. Thanks."

* * *

The detectives were back in the interview room a few minutes later.

"Well gentlemen, we are going to release you pending further enquiries," Cathal Waters said to the two suspects who had been brought up from their cells to where the desk sergeant had booked them in earlier.

"How are we going to get back to Cork?" Danny Roche said.

"We might be able to get you train tickets, but not until tomorrow. You wouldn't believe the paperwork that we have to complete to get a travel voucher around here."

"For fuck's sake! That's no use to me," Roche said.

Cathal Waters just shrugged. When it became clear that the Gardaí were not going to assist further, the two men collected their bits and pieces and marched out of the station muttering expletives under their breath.

They left the station and walked down to Mulgannon Road via Rocks Lane, turning right towards the town centre. When they had got well clear of the Garda premises, Roche stopped, looked around, and took out his mobile phone, making a quick call.

Ciara Nestor was following in her own car, and was able to pull into an entrance so that she couldn't be easily seen, but was still able to observe her quarry. Roche was having some kind of animated conversation on the phone, and Defoe was throwing in the odd comment too. It didn't seem very harmonious. When Roche finally terminated the call, the two men continued to argue, to the extent that passers-by crossed the road to avoid getting caught up in what looked like a heated disagreement. Nestor called in using her radio to report the situation.

"OK, Ciara. Just stay with them and see what happens next. Are you sure you can't be seen?" Kirkby said.

"Yes, positive. They don't appear to be going anywhere, for now at least. I'll let you know if there are any developments."

"OK, thanks."

Nestor waited another fifteen minutes, wondering what was going to happen next. This was the hardest part of her new role. Just hanging around with nothing much going on. But when she was just thinking that she had been sent on a fool's errand, an old green Ford van pulled up alongside Defoe and Roche, and the passenger door opened. The two men sat in beside the driver, pulled the door closed and the van took off in a puff of blue exhaust smoke.

Nestor started her own car, and making sure there was at least two vehicles between her and the van, she followed on while using her radio to alert the others.

"Suspects have been picked up by a green van, registration 98WD70409, and are heading out of town by the looks of it," Nestor said into the radio.

"OK, Ciara. Once it's clear which route they are taking, let us know and we'll fall in behind you."

"Roger."

A few minutes later, Nestor was back on the radio.

"Suspects now headed west on the N25 towards New Ross. I'm keeping a safe distance and I don't think I've been spotted."

"OK, Ciara," Kirkby said, "well done. We'll take over at Larkin's Cross, and you can fall back. Then if they are still on the N25 when we get to Ballinruan, you can overtake us and keep up the surveillance. OK?"

"Yes, understood. What car are you using?" Nestor said.

"We're in my pale blue car – 191D77224."

"Fine, see you in a while then."

Despite the rather dilapidated condition of the green van – it had only one light working, and it was grimy and quite bashed up – it managed a reasonable speed, though the driver was careful not to exceed the limit. As they approached Larkin's Cross, Nestor saw Kirkby's blue car approaching in her rear-view mirror, and she slowed down to let it past. She then allowed a further two vehicles to get in between herself and her colleagues, and as far as the green van was concerned, she would have disappeared from view altogether.

At Ballinruan, as arranged, Ciara Nestor put on a spurt and overtook several cars, including Kirkby's, to position herself once again in sight of the green van. Before they got to Ballinaboola, the van suddenly turned left onto a narrow lane without signalling, and Nestor had to brake sharply to avoid overshooting the turn.

She followed it down the single-track road, and could just see the van swinging into a large, concrete yard with several long three-axle trailers parked in front of an enormous metal barn. Nestor pulled her car into a gateway and managed to mount the rough grass and hide her vehicle behind the hedge.

"Full stop, full stop," she said into the radio. "Suspects have turned into a large yard just up ahead. I don't think I've been seen. I'm going to decamp and see if I can get a bit closer on foot."

"Be careful, Ciara," Kirkby said, but Nestor had already signed off.

Chapter Thirty-Four

Nestor made her way stealthily up along the hedge that was protecting her from view towards the yard. When she got close, she could see that the three men she had been following had been joined by a fourth man. The new arrival was dressed in a smart business suit, and was standing beside an almost new BMW 7 Series that was gleaming in the lights that were positioned all around the huge shed.

Nestor wanted to hear what was being said, so she edged her way ever closer to the men, doing her best to stay well hidden by the undergrowth. When she was just about in earshot, she hunkered down to eavesdrop on their conversation.

* * *

Kirkby and Waters had parked their car at the end of the lane leading to the yard.

"I know this place," Kirkby said. "I've been here before. It's where they refurbish the trailers that come in from England, and change the identification plates. But I don't like the idea that Ciara is exposed."

Without saying a word, Waters took out his mobile phone and dialled Nestor's number.

* * *

Nestor's phone started ringing in her pocket. To her, it sounded extremely loud in the silence all around her, and as soon as it started to ring, the man in the suit looked over in her direction.

"What the fuck?" he shouted.

He nodded at Defoe, who sprinted across the yard and into the bushes, almost tripping over Nestor who was trying to make herself invisible.

"Gotcha, you little bitch," he said grabbing her roughly, and twisting her left arm up painfully behind her back. He marched her over to where the other men were standing.

"Well, well, who have we here?" Daniel Roche said.

With no reply forthcoming, Defoe tweaked Nestor's arm roughly.

"I'm a Detective Garda," Nestor said rather sheepishly.

"Is she on her own?" the suited man said.

"I think so. Are ye, sweetie?" Defoe said.

"Yes. I followed you from Wexford. But there's no one else with me," she said.

"Silly cow. Put her in one of the trailers and make sure it's properly locked up. Take her phone from her first, and tie her up with cable ties. Oh, and turn the fridge unit on. That'll cool her ardour for her," the suit instructed.

Earl Defoe started to argue.

"No one said nothing about killing a cop," he protested.

The suit looked him coldly in the eye.

"Do as you're told," he said, "or so help me, I'll drop you where you stand."

Defoe dragged Nestor over to the vehicle, threw her in, locked the door and started the Thermo King unit that would cool the insides to a very uncomfortable four degrees in a matter of hours.

Kirkby and Waters were near enough to see their colleague being manhandled into one of the huge trailers, but not close enough to hear what was being said.

"Well done, Cathal. That was bloody clever," Kirkby hissed.

"Sorry, boss," Waters replied sheepishly.

"Get back to the car and summon back-up. Tell them one of ours had been captured and her life may be in danger. Don't hold back. I want the Armed Support Unit out here as fast as they can get here, and anyone else who is available!"

Waters slunk off back the way they had come, making sure that he couldn't be seen from the yard.

When Earl Defoe rejoined the little group, the well-dressed man started barking orders.

"You two better get out of here. And don't you dare go anywhere near Cork. They'll be watching that place like hawks. Fuck off to Dublin or something and lay low for a while. I'll call you when this all settles down. We have a lot of unfinished business."

"What about the cop woman?" Roche asked.

"What about her? She isn't going anywhere, is she?" he replied.

The man opened the rear door of the BMW and slid into the car's sumptuous pale leather seats. Kirkby realised that there must be a driver, as the car began to move off.

Kirkby called Cathal Waters on the radio.

"Cathal. Pull the car across the road. There's a black BMW heading your way, and it needs to be stopped. Do whatever," she barked into her radio.

"Right, boss. Understood."

But instead of turning left out of the yard, the BMW went right, continuing on down the single-track road at high speed, throwing up gravel and dust as it disappeared around a bend.

"Shit!" Kirkby said out loud, and a second later she was back on the radio.

"Cathal. Get here now. The fucker has gone the other way. Pick me up as you go past."

Waters manoeuvred Kirkby's car to face back towards the yard.

"Make your bloody mind up, woman," he said to himself as he twisted the steering wheel this way and that to turn the car in the very limited space.

As he drove back to collect his boss, the old green van appeared in front of him. There simply wasn't room for the two vehicles to pass, and the van didn't look like it was going to give way. It came on at speed, its single working headlight flashing in Waters' face as it thundered towards him. At the last second before the inevitable impact, Waters spun the steering wheel, and the little car obediently mounted the ditch and fell into the deep ravine alongside the road, its engine screaming. The van clipped the side of Waters' car as it left the road, but carried on, and was out of sight within seconds.

Waters was a bit woozy after the incident, but conscious, and wasn't hurt. He clicked the transmit button on his radio.

"Sorry, boss, they got away," he said sheepishly.

"Fuck, fuck, fuck! What about back-up? Are they anywhere nearby?"

"I don't know, boss. Will I give them a call?"

"Why not, Cathal? And see if they are close enough to snag the two absconders while you're at it. Tell them to get a helicopter up if needs be. We can't let this lot get away."

Kirkby walked back into the yard where the trailers were stored. The only one that was locked contained Ciara Nestor, and Kirkby knew she had to get her out of there, and soon. The place appeared to be deserted, but the door to the workshop was still open, so Kirkby made her way inside, watching carefully in case there was anyone still there. She went to the workbench that was positioned up along the left-hand side of the huge enclosure. After a bit of rummaging, she found a bolt cutter. She wasn't entirely sure how to use it, or whether it would be strong enough to sever the padlock that was keeping her colleague incarcerated, but she had to give it her best shot.

Back outside, she placed the hasp of the lock into the jaws of the tool and squeezed, but she simply didn't have enough strength to make any impression on the lock.

Waters, who had abandoned the car in the ditch as it was undriveable, walked up behind her.

"Here. Let me try," he said, taking hold of the long arms of the bolt cutter. He drew in his breath, and summoning all the strength the muscles in his arms would provide. He squeezed hard, with his hands at the very end of the handles to maximize leverage. After two attempts during which his face had gone an alarming colour somewhere between red and purple, a satisfying click was heard, and the lock swung free from the door closures.

Kirkby wasted no time in opening the trailer wide, and getting Ciara Nestor out. Waters helped her down from the load area, and used the bolt cutter again to release the tie wraps around her wrists and ankles.

"Wow. Thanks, guys. It was getting a mighty bit chilly in there," Nestor said, rubbing her wrists which now had red welts around them from the plastic restraints.

"What's the story with the men who were here?" Nestor said.

"They've all scarpered," Kirkby said, looking vexed at her detective sergeant. "We'll have to wait for back-up. They should be here soon."

Nestor had the good sense to say nothing.

Chapter Thirty-Five

The back-up team that Waters had called in, figured that the man in the suit would be keen to get out of the area as quickly as possible. To do that, he would have to continue down the lane that ran outside the trailer yard for a few kilometres, then turn left, and weave his way back onto the N25, rejoining it near Larkin's Cross. At that point, he could choose to go back towards Wexford, and then take the N11 to Dublin, or perhaps he would stick to the narrow lanes to avoid detection. They had a description of the vehicle and the registration number of the BMW from Kirkby, so they positioned two unmarked Ford Mondeos at the petrol station that was just off the roundabout at Larkin's Cross, and waited.

Sure enough, it wasn't long before the sleek saloon came into view. The two unmarked cars pulled out of the petrol station. One of the Mondeos fell in behind the BMW, while the other one overtook it and, with blue lights and sirens activated, gently eased the car onto the hard shoulder. Three burly Gardaí dressed in anti-stab vests and holding Glock 17 pistols surrounded the BMW and pulled open the back doors.

The biggest of the Gardaí uttered a simple, one-word instruction.

"Out," he said, pointing his weapon at the man in the suit.

The man obeyed, and stood obligingly with his hands behind his back so that another of the Gardaí snapped handcuffs on him.

The first officer issued another single word instruction. "Name."

The man said nothing, so the lead Garda reached into the suspect's inside jacket pocket and withdrew a wallet. He opened it to reveal several credit and debit cards and a UK driving license in the name of Leonard Walker. The photograph on the license left the officer in no doubt as to the man's identity.

"Leonard Walker, I'm arresting you on suspicion of the abduction of a serving member of An Garda Síochána in the execution of her duty. You do not have to say anything, but anything you do say may be taken down and used in evidence against you."

As they stood there going through the motions of the arrest, a white Transit van pulled up alongside. The arresting officer opened the rear of the van which was laid out like a small prison cell, and assisted Leonard Walker to take a seat within. He slammed the door loudly, and gave a signal to the driver to move on.

The driver of the BMW had also been arrested by this time as an accessory, and was handcuffed and placed in the back seat of his car accompanied by another burly officer. One of the other Gardaí sat into the driver's seat of the BMW, setting off in convoy with the two Mondeos. The whole process had taken less than five minutes to complete.

Defoe, Roche, and the driver of the green van hadn't fared so well. They were very keen to get away from the site as soon as they could, and the somewhat basic skills of the driver and the decrepit state of their vehicle conspired to cause them to leave the road at some speed and hit a stone wall at a bend. The van more or less disintegrated. The driver came off worst. His head hit the A post of the old van with such ferocity that he was killed instantly. Defoe and Roche were thrown around inside the van, and while they sustained some pretty bad cuts about their faces, and Roche managed to break his arm, their injuries were not life-threatening.

A local farmer witnessed the mêlée, and called 999. With a heavy Garda presence in the area, it wasn't long before they arrived at the scene and arrested Roche and Defoe, whilst summoning an ambulance to take all three fugitives back to the hospital in Wexford.

News came across the airwaves to Kirkby, Nestor and Waters.

"Well, that's that then," Kirkby said. "Let's go and find your car, Ciara, and get back to the nick. Are you OK to drive?"

"Yeah, no bother. I'm looking forward to the next bit," Nestor said, grinning broadly.

* * *

"Come in, Inspector, take a seat. I hear you've been having some adventures out in the countryside," Frawley said with a broad grin on his face. "Mind you, you've probably burnt off half a year's worth of budget with that little caper. Tell me you've got someone for the murder of Mr and Mrs Roche?"

"There's no doubt, sir, that we have uncovered a major organised crime operation involving VAT fraud and the falsification of documents associated with the illegal importation of road vehicles. It seems this is a widespread operation, involving activity in both Cork and Rosslare, with the proceeds running to millions of euros, and involving some very nasty types."

"Yes, yes, that's all very well. We'll be handing that over to Organised Crime for them to sort out, and I'm sure they'll be eternally grateful. But what about the murders?" Frawley said, visibly finding it difficult to hide his frustration.

"We have Daniel Roche in custody, sir, and I believe he knows a lot more about it than he has told us so far. His behaviour is very suspicious, and he has a lot of unexplained wealth too. And he's definitely involved in the lorry smuggling. I have proof of that," Kirkby said.

"But surely, you're not suggesting that he murdered his father and his mother. Even for you, Inspector, that's a bit of a leap, is it not?"

"I'll know more when I have interviewed him, sir. And I may have to ask for an extension to his detention."

"Jesus, Inspector. I hope you're right about this. You'd better go and get on with it then, and be sure to keep me posted. I don't want to hear from someone else, do you understand?"

"Yes, sir. Of course, sir."

* * *

"OK, Cathal. Will you go with Ciara and interview Mr Smooth in the suit. Don't be too gentle with him. I want him well and truly rattled. And don't take any crap from his brief either. This is a double murder after all, and I need some answers. Got it?" Kirkby said.

"Yes, OK, boss. Are you going to interview Roche?"

"Damn right I am, and by the time I'm finished with him, he'll wish he hadn't been found in the truck!"

Waters and Nestor watched their boss stalk off down the hallway. Waters said to Ciara Nestor in a quiet tone, "Blimey, I wonder what raw meat she had for breakfast?"

Nestor just rolled her eyes to heaven.

* * *

When Daniel Roche arrived at the hospital, he was taken directly to the accident and emergency department where he was seen almost immediately by a very friendly doctor. His cuts were dressed – they weren't serious in any case, just a bit unpleasant-looking, but when his broken arm was discovered, he was whisked away to an operating theatre where he underwent an anaesthetic to have the bones set in place, and a stiff cast wrapped around the break. He spent the night in the hospital, but was released the following morning back into Garda custody feeling very sorry for himself. It was in this hapless state that Kirkby found him when she entered the interview room carrying a cardboard cup of strong coffee.

"Well now, Mr Roche, you have been in the wars, haven't you?" she said, taking a seat opposite the man who looked crestfallen and dejected.

He just grunted in reply.

Kirkby read the usual mantra and asked if Roche would like a solicitor present. He declined.

"Right. OK, now I want you to tell me what the hell is going on here. Take me from the time you were discovered tied up in the front of the Tiverton lorry."

Roche looked pitifully at the inspector. He was visibly shaken, and at one point Kirkby thought he might burst into tears.

"I'm the victim here, Inspector. Don't you see, they want me dead."

"Who wants you dead, Daniel, and why?"

"I can't say. They'll probably do for me in any case now, but if I grass on them, I won't last till teatime."

"Well, that's hardly true, is it? You're in Garda custody. No one can get to you in here, unless of course we release you, which I may have to do if you don't start talking."

Kirkby knew that this wasn't true, but she needed to get the man to open up, otherwise they would only have a few minor charges to get him into court, and he would almost certainly be bailed by the judge and abscond.

"Looks like I'm done for whatever way it goes then," Roche said.

"Not necessarily. Look, we know you're involved somehow in this smuggling and VAT fraud thing that's going on. But to be brutally honest, I don't give a damn about that. It will be taken out of my hands in any case. Organised Crime will be working that one. My concern is the murder of your parents. So, let's focus on that for a few minutes."

Kirkby paused for a moment and took a sip of her coffee which was now only lukewarm, but she wanted to let what she had said sink in.

"You see, I think you lied to us about the night your folks were killed. I believe you were at the property shortly before they were shot, and the fact that you told us otherwise makes me very suspicious. What was all that about?"

"I didn't kill them, I swear. I couldn't. They were good people," Roche said.

"OK, I hear you. But someone did, and I think you probably know who. So why don't you get it off your chest. You'll feel better and I'll be able to pursue the real killers and get them behind bars," Kirkby said.

Roche remained silent, looking down at the table that stood between them, saying nothing.

"C'mon, Daniel. This won't do. You need to start talking."

Roche looked up at Vikki Kirkby.

"It's Leonard Walker you need to be talking to. He's the one behind all this, and he knows who killed them. But for God's sake, don't tell him I told you. These are not nice people you're dealing with."

"OK. I'll be talking to Mr Walker later. But in the meantime, I want you to tell me what exactly is happening with those vehicles."

Chapter Thirty-Six

"It's a very simple scam, Inspector. The trucks come over from the UK just like lots of others with cargo for Ireland. They drop off their loads, and then the trailers are taken to that place out by Newbawn and left there. The lads refurbish the wagons, give them a new, local, identity, and put them up for sale. They make about twenty or twenty-five grand profit on each one, and they don't pay any import duties or VAT. But this is not just in Wexford. They have this operation going on all over Ireland and the UK. They bring trailers from all over Europe where they are much cheaper and flog them as new or nearly new. It's a multi-million-euro wheeze, and up to now, no one has been any the wiser."

"So, what role to do you play in all of this, Danny?"

"They need a few friends in Customs and Excise to smooth the way. When the trailers don't go back on the ferries, we have to alter the records to cover their tracks."

"So, there would be crooked customs officials at each of the ports doing this then?"

"Yes. It's not difficult to find them. They are not generally well paid, and lots of them have some backstory that they'd prefer to keep quiet about, so between bribery and blackmail, they can be fairly easily turned."

"How was your father involved?"

"He wasn't. But he was very observant, and working day in, day out at the port he soon figured that there was something iffy going on with Tiverton Transport. When he made it known that he was on to them, they started to pay him to keep quiet. But when that became known further up the food chain, they weren't happy, and said he had to be silenced. I thought they were just going to warn him off. I had no idea they were going to kill him, honestly."

"Was that why your dad was keeping all those records?"

"Yes, he felt it gave him some insurance in case things went bad."

"Do you happen to know if Peter Booth was in any way involved with the scam, Danny?"

"I couldn't say. But I've heard a few things."

"Like what?"

"They say he's a bit handy with his fists. I heard a rumour that he was some kind of enforcer here in Rosslare for the gang, but nothing specific."

"I see."

This wasn't good news for Vikki Kirkby.

"What did your father do with the money he received?" Kirkby asked, needing to change the subject rapidly.

"That's the mad thing. You'd think he'd spend a bit on himself or Mam. You know, do the house up, or have a nicer holiday. But no. My mother used to give it all away to that school she worked in. They were constantly broke, and she wanted to help them out."

"I see."

"And he had quite a bit saved up. I think that was for his retirement. He didn't want to work until he dropped, like his father had."

"OK. Well, look, Danny, I'm going to have to keep you here and we'll need to ask you some more questions later on. And our Organised Crime people will want time with you too. And if I can't get any sense out of Walker, you may still be on the hook for the murder of your parents. Understood?"

Roche just buried his face in his hands and said nothing.

* * *

When Kirkby got back upstairs, Cathal Waters and Ciara Nestor were sitting at Nestor's desk chatting.

"What's the story with yer man?" Kirkby asked them.

"He's all lawyered up and 'no comment', boss," Waters said. "How did you get on?"

"Just peachy, Cathal. Roche has admitted – well more or less – to his involvement in the VAT scam. We need to turn all that over to Organised Crime. Can you get all our papers together and I'll see if Frawley can get someone down from Dublin this afternoon to take over that part of the investigation. But I want a few minutes with Mr Walker before that. He's up to his neck in this whole thing, and I think he knows who killed the Roches too, if he didn't do it himself."

Waters whispered under his breath, "Good luck with that."

"Ciara, will you take Defoe? We don't even know where he's from. When you find out, get onto the UK police and see if he has a record. With a bit of luck there may even be a warrant out for him. See what the story is and let me know if there's anything interesting," Kirkby said. "And, Cathal, I want you to do some digging on Leonard Walker. See what you can find out about him."

"Right, boss," they both responded in unison.

Kirkby went back downstairs to where Walker was seated with his brief, talking quietly. The solicitor Walker had retained was not your usual duty solicitor, who were often young trainees with little interest in their clients, and little knowledge of the law surrounding arrests. They were often there purely for show, but not this time. This one was a woman, which in itself was somewhat unusual outside Dublin, and she spoke in a well-educated accent. She was immaculately turned out in a navy-blue business suit with a white cotton blouse, and her dark chestnut-coloured hair that hung to her shoulders had seen the inside of a salon very recently, Kirkby calculated.

Standing up when Kirkby entered the room, the solicitor introduced herself.

"I'm Jennifer Russell, from Russell and Dunne. I'm representing Mr Walker today, and if I may say, I think he has been treated very badly so far."

"Hello, Ms Russell. Perhaps you'd like to take a seat so we can get on."

Before they were seated – Walker hadn't got up at all – Russell said, "Why exactly is my client here, Inspector? He has important business matters to see to and this is to say the least a terrific nuisance."

"Indeed. Just to put you in the picture, Ms Russell, your client drove off at high speed, or should I say, his driver did, when we were about to interview him at the yard up at Newbawn where we believe serious crimes are being committed. He was also involved in the kidnap of a serving officer, and he was in the company of others who have also been taken into custody, and are being questioned right now," Kirkby said, not taking her eyes off the cold blue gaze of her adversary.

"So, perhaps Mr Walker could tell me why he was there and what his business is with these people. And remember, we have the testimony of a serving member of the force saying that it was your client who instructed her to be locked away in the fridge unit," Kirkby said.

"My client denies he said anything of the kind, and he has witnesses who will back him up. So, have you any actual evidence tying Mr Walker to whatever you think is going on out there?" Russell said.

"I'd like to know what Mr Walker was doing at the yard where one of my officers was assaulted. What exactly is his business, and what is his involvement with Tiverton Transport?"

"I'm not happy, Inspector, that you have solid evidential grounds to detain my client. Come on, Mr Walker, let's get out of here," she said, as she stood up, indicating that Walker should do the same.

"Not so fast. Until I am satisfied that there is a sensible explanation for why your client was where we found him, and why he absconded at high speed, not to mention the kidnap of one of my officers, he's going nowhere. So, I'll give you a few minutes to confer, and then I'll be needing some answers." With that, Kirkby stood up, turned her back on them, and left the room.

As Kirkby walked back down along the corridor to where Earl Defoe was being interviewed by Ciara Nestor, her phone pinged in her pocket. It was a message from Keith Sexton in forensics asking her to call him.

She dialled his number.

"Hi, Keith, what's up?"

"Hello, Inspector. You brought a man in earlier by the name of Earl Defoe. He was fingerprinted at the desk when he was booked in, and it popped up here on my system as he may be connected to an active investigation. Well, I did some checking, and we have a print from the man himself that we recovered from the Roches' house where the two people were shot. There's only one dab that we found on the kitchen door jamb, but it's definitely a match, 95% certainty."

"I see. That's interesting. Thanks, Keith. Send over the report as soon as you can. We have Mr Defoe here for the next little while."

"Great. It's on its way."

Kirkby entered the room where Ciara Nestor was interviewing Earl Defoe. Nestor added the required narrative to the recording, and Kirkby sat down beside her.

"Mr Defoe was just telling me that he's just a driver for Tiverton. He knows nothing about anything, really. He just goes where he's told, and gets badly paid for his efforts."

Kirkby stared at Defoe for what seemed like an age, till he eventually averted his gaze.

"That's not entirely true, now Earl, is it?"

"What do you mean?" he asked.

"I've just been speaking to our forensic people. They tell me that they found a nice clear fingerprint on the door frame at the house where Mr and Mrs Roche were murdered. And guess what, Earl? It's yours."

Defoe said nothing for a moment, then he leaned forward and buried his face in his hands. No one spoke.

After several minutes had passed, Defoe eventually said, "I think I need a solicitor."

Kirkby nodded to Nestor, and the two of them got up to leave the room.

"We'll get you a duty solicitor, Earl. We'll be back in a while."

Chapter Thirty-Seven

Kirkby, Nestor and Waters were all back in Kirkby's office a few minutes later.

"OK, Cathal," Kirkby said, "what did you find out about our friend Walker downstairs?"

"Interesting. He's listed as a non-executive director of Tiverton Transport, but his main business seems to be as a financial advisor of some kind. There are a few rumours on social media about him being involved in some dodgy doings, so I've put a request in to the UK Serious Fraud Office to see what they may have on him, if anything," Waters said.

"Excellent. Have you a named contact over there?"

"Yes, they responded saying that an Inspector Montgomery would be dealing with my enquiry."

"Good stuff."

Kirkby filled Waters in on what had been discovered about Defoe's fingerprint at the Roches' house.

"Cripes. What are you going to do now, boss?" Waters said.

"I'm going back to talk to Danny. I think he may spill the beans when I tell him about the new evidence. Ciara, will you stick with Defoe when his solicitor turns up?"

"Sure, boss, but if we're going to charge him with murder, I'll need some help."

"Of course!"

* * *

It wasn't long before Inspector Ian Montgomery from the UK's Serious Fraud Office called Cathal Waters.

"Hello, Sergeant Waters. I believe you are making enquiries about a Leonard Walker, is that right?"

"Yes, that's it, Inspector."

"Just to be sure we have the right person, has this Mr Walker got anything to do with Tiverton Transport, as far as you are aware?" Montgomery said.

"The very one, Inspector. Do you know of him?"

"Indeed, I do, Sergeant. I don't suppose you know where the man is at this moment, do you?"

"As a matter of fact, I do. He's currently enjoying our hospitality here at Wexford Garda headquarters. He's in a nice uncomfortable cell as we speak."

"Excellent. We've been looking for Walker for some time. We need to interview him about a series of financial irregularities here in England. What have you got him in for?" Montgomery said.

"It's a long and complex story, Inspector. But let's just say there is a double murder we are investigating, and what looks like a series of VAT scams to do with illegally imported three-axle road trailers."

"I see. I wouldn't have thought he was into violent crime, Sergeant, but the VAT thing sounds about right. We have some information here ourselves on that, and that's just part of what we think he's been up to. So, how do you think we can progress this?"

"Well, it's a bit tricky since you left the EU. If you were still in, you could use a European Arrest Warrant, but I'm not sure exactly what the protocol is now," Waters said.

"Hmm. I was hoping we might be able to do something a little less formal, Sergeant. Do you think that might be possible?"

"I'm not sure, sir. I'd need to consult with our SIO, Detective Inspector Kirkby."

"OK. But do you think that you'll be able to talk to him before you have to release Walker?" Montgomery said, making the usual assumption that DI Kirkby was a man.

"It's *her*, Inspector. DI Kirkby is a woman."

"Oh, sorry. I just assumed…"

"No worries. If you give me your direct line, I'll call you back as soon as I have something."

"Yes, sure, but can you be certain Walker won't be released?" Montgomery said.

"Oh, don't worry on that score. He's not going anywhere anytime soon."

"Fair enough."

Montgomery reeled off a phone number which Waters took down and then read back to the man.

"That's it, Sergeant. I'll wait to hear from you."

* * *

Vikki Kirkby was just about to get started with Danny Roche when Waters caught her outside the interview room. He told her about the call he had taken from the UK.

"That's excellent, Cathal. I didn't think we had a very strong motive to hold that geezer anyway. It's all a bit circumstantial. And he's a right smoothie. But if we can find a way to introduce him to the Brits, that should take care of him. Have we anything back from our own Organised Crime lot?"

"I'll check that up now, boss. I think they're on the way down here with a few officers to secure the yard. They may want a word with Mr Walker too."

"Hmm. Ok, let me get on with Roche junior and see what develops."

"OK. Catch you later, boss."

Kirkby went into the interview room where Danny Roche was seated, looking rather wrung out, alongside the duty solicitor.

No sooner had she taken a seat and read the obligatory notice into the recorder, than the solicitor piped up.

"My client would like to make a statement, Inspector."

"Very well. Let's hear what he has to say," Kirkby responded, not very hopefully.

"Before he does, I want you to understand that my client feels that his personal safety may be in jeopardy. As you know, he has already had what could be described as a narrow escape, and he needs some reassurance that arrangements will be made to protect him."

"Let's see what he has to say first, shall we? Then I'll see what I can do."

The solicitor looked at Danny Roche and nodded slightly.

Danny Roche looked up and rubbed his eyes. "I didn't kill them. I couldn't. But I am so deep in with this mob, that I had to do what they told me to do, otherwise it would have been me getting both barrels in my chest. So, I drove the killer up from Cork and waited outside the house until the job was done. I was sick to my stomach, but I had no choice. He went inside. I heard two loud bangs and then we both drove off at speed back to Cork. I didn't even ask if they were dead." With that, Danny Roche broke down and sobbed loudly.

Kirkby gave him a few minutes to compose himself.

"Who was it that actually pulled the trigger?" Kirkby said.

"Defoe. He's a weak man, and very motivated by money. He'll do anything he is told, provided the price is right."

"How did he get the gun?"

"It was smuggled in on one of the lorries in a consignment of vegetables that came from Spain. We get quite a lot of stuff in like that. I'm in charge of the inspections, so I can easily let stuff through."

At this revelation, the solicitor touched Danny's arm and shook his head from side to side silently.

"It's OK. I'm honestly glad to be getting all this off my chest. None of this is who I am. Not really," Roche said, tearfully.

"Who is behind this whole thing, Danny? The trailers, the smuggling, the violence?"

"I don't know. Walker is my only contact with the gang, apart from some of the drivers and the lads out at the yard at Newbawn. We're told very little. But it's a very big operation. I heard Walker on the phone one time when he was over here before. I think he was talking to someone in Latvia, or somewhere like that."

When Kirkby decided that Danny Roche had nothing more of interest to divulge, she advised both him and his brief that they would be charging Danny with accessory to murder, conspiracy to murder, and various other smuggling and fraud-related charges yet to be determined. She then got up and left the room.

Chapter Thirty-Eight

"Cathal, I need to speak to that Inspector Montgomery. Can I have his number?" Kirkby said.

"Sure, boss. Here it is," Waters said, handing her a slip of paper. But he was a little miffed that she was acquiring the contact he had made.

Kirkby sensed what Waters was thinking.

"Don't worry, Cathal, I'm not going to eat your lunch. We'll call him from my office on speakerphone, so you can join in whenever you want to."

"Thanks, boss," Waters said with a slight smile, walking behind her into the office.

"Come in, Cathal. Close the door."

When they were both seated, Kirkby switched on the desk telephone speaker and dialled the UK number. The phone at the other end was answered after two rings.

"Montgomery."

"Hello, Inspector. My name is Vikki Kirkby I'm the DI from the Wexford Detective Unit. You were speaking to my colleague earlier, DS Cathal Waters, about our mutual friend Leonard Walker."

"Oh, yes. Hello, Inspector. Thanks for calling. I understand you have Walker in custody."

"Yes, that's right, and a couple of his goons too, one of whom goes by the name of Earl Defoe. Our specialist team is on the way from Dublin as we speak to take over the whole business of the VAT scam and the trailers. I'm more interested in a murder that seems to be tied up with this whole thing," Kirkby said.

"Yes, my colleagues have been speaking to your people. We were just about to launch a major Europe-wide operation to round up the entire gang – or however many of them we can. This thing is pretty extensive. It reaches across much of Europe, the UK and Ireland too it seems. We've brought the operation forward based on what took place over there."

"I see. Well, that's good news. I'm not sure exactly how this will all finish up just yet. I need to interview Earl Defoe again. One of his associates has said that it was him who actually shot two innocent people here on orders from the gang."

"Earl Defoe. Let me see if we have anything on him here. Hang on a second, I'll look up our system."

Kirkby and Waters listened as Montgomery clicked away on his keyboard.

"Ah, yes. We do indeed have information on Mr Defoe. Gracious, he's a nasty piece of work. He's done time for GBH over here, and the French are looking for him in connection with an arson attack on a home where there was a mother and two young children inside. I'd say they'd be very grateful to hear that you have him locked up."

"Well, if our information is correct, the French will have to wait a good few years to get their hands on him. But listen, it sounds to me that you have the VAT scam well in hand. I'm going to hand that over to our serious crime squad now, and focus on wrapping up the murder enquiry. Is there anything else I can do for you over here, Inspector?" Kirkby said.

"No, I think it's all in hand. As usual with these cases, the people behind the whole thing will probably get away to fight another day. But at least we will disrupt their operation for a while at least. Thanks for your help," Montgomery said.

"And you for yours. OK. So just let me know if there's anything else we can do to help. Bye."

When the call was finished, Kirkby turned to Cathal Waters.

"Right, Cathal. Did you get all the paperwork together on this bloody nonsense with the trailers?"

"Yes, boss."

"Good. Well find out who is in charge of the case from our side and pass it all over. I want to hand over as much of this as we can."

"What are you going to do, boss?"

"I'm going to find Ciara Nestor and see if we can't get a confession out of Defoe."

* * *

Vikki Kirkby and Ciara Nestor went to interview Earl Defoe. He had equipped himself with a solicitor, but the detectives gleaned from the man's demeanour that he wasn't too interested in his client. He was more or less just going through the motions.

"OK, Earl. I want you to tell me about the evening that Daniel Roche drove you from Cork to his parents' house in Tobinstown," Kirkby said looking Defoe directly in the eye.

"No comment," came the surly reply.

"All right. We can do this the hard way if you prefer, Earl, but you should know that we have a witness statement that says that you murdered Danny Roche's parents in cold blood on that evening, and we have forensic evidence tying you to the crime scene too. So, it would be in your best interests to tell us what you know."

Defoe smirked and looked at Kirkby.

"He'll never get to testify."

"Ah, well now you see, I think you could be wrong there. After all, you tried to get rid of Danny once before, didn't you? And that didn't end well."

"Hmph," Defoe grunted, but he wasn't grinning any longer.

"Why did you do it, Earl? Were you being threatened?"

At this, the solicitor decided he had better earn his keep and interjected to say, "You don't have to answer that, Mr Defoe."

"It's OK, bro, it's cool. No, actually, I volunteered. It was a blast – in more ways than one." He chuckled at his own sick joke.

"So, you are admitting to shooting Mr and Mrs Roche at their home in Tobinstown then. Is that correct?"

The solicitor was looking very uneasy.

"Whatever," Defoe replied, shrugging his shoulders.

"I'll take that as affirmative then," Kirkby said, looking at her colleague.

"Where did you get the weapon?" Nestor asked, now that the suspect was in a more talkative mood.

"It came in on the boat. We've got connections right across Europe, you know. We get all sorts of stuff through there. Your customs people ain't up to much, is they?"

Defoe's solicitor seemed to have given up. He said nothing, but just continued to look unhappy.

"And apart from being a hired killer for this gang, whoever they are, what else do you do for them, Earl?" Nestor continued.

Defoe just shrugged.

Kirkby looked at Nestor and nodded towards the door. The two detectives got up and left the room, saying nothing further.

As they opened the door, Defoe called after them, "Can I go now then?" he said.

"In your dreams, mate," Nestor said.

Once they were out of earshot, Kirkby said to Nestor, "Can you finish up here, Ciara? Charge him with murder and see if you can get him into court this evening. We'll be opposing bail on the basis that he's a flight risk. The judge should be happy enough with that seeing as it is a double murder. Tell him that there will be further charges to follow. We might get him on kidnapping as well, depending on whether Danny wants to press charges."

"OK, boss. I think Frawley is looking for you, by the way."

"Good. I'm looking forward to that!" Kirkby hurried off.

Chapter Thirty-Nine

Kirkby climbed the stairs to the superintendent's office with a spring in her step. She finally felt that she had reason to prove him wrong in his assessment of her, and to counter the negative information that had come down ahead of her from Dublin.

She knocked at his door, and waited. After a moment or two, she was summoned inside.

"Come in, Vikki. Take a seat. Would you like a tea of a coffee?" Frawley said.

"No thanks, sir, I'm fine."

"Well, it seems you have some good news for me, is that right?"

"Yes, sir. The team and I have solved the double murder of the Roches. We have one Earl Defoe in custody, and he'll be going to court later. The son is also in the frame for conspiracy to murder, and quite a few other charges to do with smuggling and VAT evasion. We have another couple of men to be charged too, but I'm leaving that to our colleagues from Organised Crime," Kirkby said, without pausing for breath.

"Quite a coup then, all in all. Well done, Vikki, well done. You know I may have misjudged you initially. I've been doing a bit of digging while you were out catching that lot. It seems your rapid exit from Dublin was somewhat of a cover-up to protect another officer. Nothing can be done about that now, of course, but it puts a different light on things. How did Waters get on?"

"At first, I thought he was a bit of a dud to be honest, sir, but as the investigation progressed, he shaped up nicely. I think he'll make a good detective given the right leadership. And, if I may say so, Ciara Nestor who we had co-opted from uniform shows a lot of promise too," Kirkby said.

"Hmm. I hear you. Would you like me to see if I can make her temporary assignment to the Detective Unit permanent? Terry Lucy isn't coming back. He's retiring on the sick, I'm afraid."

"Yes, thank you, sir, I think that would be very helpful. But if I could just ask if you could let me tell her when you have it in place. That would be a great help to me in building the team."

"I think we can manage that, but don't say anything till I give you the word. Understood?" Frawley said.

"Yes, of course, sir."

"Right, well I'm sure you have work to do, Vikki. Let me know when it's all tied up and we might all go and have a drink to your success with the rest of the team."

"Thank you. I'm sure they would appreciate that. May I ask you one other thing, sir?"

"Yes, of course."

"Do you know if Peter Booth has had any involvement with any funny business at the port at all?"

Frawley stayed quiet for a minute, thinking how best to answer the woman.

"Mr Booth has been, shall we say, helpful to us with a few things. He has been involved in some criminal activity out at the port, but he's been on our side, not on the side of the villains. He provides us with some good information from time to time, and to do that, he sometimes has to do things that we'd rather he didn't. But to date it has always paid off, so we turn a blind eye. Are you still seeing him?" Frawley said.

"No, not at the moment. But that's useful to know. I suppose you are aware that he clocked a parking warden in Wexford at one stage. I don't like men that hit women," Kirkby said.

"He didn't. That was all part of a cover story to make him more attractive to the lowlife. As far as I know he's the perfect gentleman. I'm sorry I couldn't tell you earlier, but I didn't want to compromise his position," Frawley said, smiling just a little.

"I see. Thanks for sharing that with me in any case, sir. It will go no further."

"You'll get used to our country ways eventually, Vikki. We're not a bad bunch really, and sometimes we have to do things differently than they would in Dublin. But as you have proven, we get results. Now, off you go."

Kirkby got up and left the office, feeling quite good about herself.

* * *

Back downstairs, things were extremely busy. The Organised Crime deputation had arrived from Dublin, and were in the process of getting a handover for Leonard Walker. They would have liked to take Daniel Roche as well, but Kirkby insisted that he would be charged in Wexford with conspiracy to murder, as well as a rake of other charges, and if he got bail, then they could have him until his trial date on the proviso that they kept him in custody.

Ciara Nestor was arriving back from court where Earl Defoe had been charged with murder. The judge had no hesitation in remanding the man, and in any case, the solicitor representing Defoe had made a very weak case for his release on bail. Nestor brough Kirkby up to date.

"I suppose I'll be heading back to uniform now that this is all over, boss?"

Kirkby looked at Nestor. She had developed a healthy respect for the young woman's talents.

"Ah, give it a few days, Ciara. There's no mad rush, is there?" Kirkby said.

"I suppose not, boss. Thanks."

When things had settled down and the office was quieter, Vikki Kirkby called Cathal Waters and Ciara Nestor into her office.

"OK, guys. I just wanted to say that Superintendent Frawley is very impressed with the way this whole thing has gone. He says we'll all go out for a celebratory drink in a few days when we've tied up the loose ends. It's quite a feather in our caps that we were able to assist in the smashing of the smuggling ring too. I imagine criminal activity at the port will cease now for a good while at least. So well done both of you. Let's make sure everything is properly recorded and all our paperwork is in order. And thanks, folks."

"We couldn't have done it without you, boss," Cathal Waters said.

"Thanks, Cathal. Now let's get on. We have a lot to finish off."

Chapter Forty

Kirkby was at home. She had managed to get away from the station a little early, and she was catching up on some much-needed housework, having changed into her scruffs to tackle the neglect of the last few weeks in the house.

The doorbell rang, and she went to answer it without thinking about her appearance. She even kept her bright yellow Marigold rubber gloves on.

When she opened the door, brushing a strand of loose hair away from her eyes, she saw Peter Booth standing there with a very expensive bunch of flowers in one hand and a bottle of wine in the other.

"Hi, stranger. What's the story?" he said.

"Christ, Peter. Sorry, I wasn't expecting anyone. Come in. Are those for me?" she said, looking at the flowers in his hand.

"Some detective you are, Vikki," Booth said, thrusting the flowers forward.

Kirkby stood back from the door, and the two of them made their way into the kitchen-diner. Booth put down the flowers and wine, and took her in his arms. She yielded to him, and they kissed slowly and passionately.

"God, look at me. I must look dreadful. Sorry," Kirkby said.

"You look pretty good to me. What about you get changed and I take you out somewhere stupidly expensive for dinner. I hear you're a bit of a celebrity up at Mulgannon."

"I wouldn't say that, Peter, but I am very hungry. Give me ten minutes to make myself respectable."

"Need any help?" he said.

"Get off!" she said, pushing him away playfully. "Plenty of time for that later."

She had a twinkle in her eye and a broad smile on her pretty face.

Epilogue

The Europe-wide police raids on Tiverton Transport had gone well. More than twenty serious criminals were taken into custody, and the smuggling and VAT frauds were essentially closed down.

The trailers out at Newbawn were sold, and the funds went to the Irish Revenue Commissioners as the proceeds of crime. The yard was closed up, and soon became completely derelict with weeds growing up through the concrete apron and holes starting to appear in the roof, letting in rain.

Daniel Roche was ultimately tried and convicted on several counts, including conspiracy to murder, and was handed down a fifteen-year sentence. His fancy house in Montenotte is being processed by the Criminal Assets Bureau who will eventually acquire it and sell it on.

Earl Defoe was convicted of the double murder of Frank and Eileen Roche. His defence was that he was acting under duress, but the jury weren't having any of it, and he got a life sentence for his trouble.

The money held in the Roches' Credit Union account should have gone to Daniel, but as you are not allowed to benefit financially from a crime that you have committed, he agreed that it should be donated to the school in Wellingtonbridge where his mother had worked. The school was delighted to accept it, as it would put them on a much sounder financial footing for some time to come.

Ciara Nestor was permanently transferred to the Detective Unit, and was delighted with the change.

Peter Booth and Kirkby continued their relationship. They grew quite fond of each other, but neither was ready to make any long-term commitment, and Kirkby, in particular, wanted to firmly establish herself in Wexford as a key member of Frawley's team. With her reputation now restored, she might even look for a transfer back to Dublin – she wasn't sure.

But what she was sure of was that Nestor, Waters and herself made a formidable team. Even Jim Kennedy had to admit that the Roche case had been a tough one, and he recognised the skill that Kirkby had used to bring the perpetrators to book.

Superintendent Frawley dined out on several occasions on the success of the case. Even the Garda commissioner recognised the achievement, and when Frawley received a letter of appreciation from the commissioner, he made good on his promise to take the team out for a slap-up meal and quite a few drinks.

But crime moves on, and in the Gardaí, to some extent at least, you're only as good as your last collar. It wouldn't be long before Kirkby and her team were challenged once again with a difficult and distressing case. Could they be as successful next time?

List of Characters

Detective Inspector Vikki Kirkby – a seasoned detective who has some scores to settle

Detective Sergeant Cathal Waters – a rather slovenly detective Garda with a lot to learn

Garda Ciara Nestor – an ambitious young Garda

Detective Superintendent Liam Frawley – a tough senior officer in charge of the Detective Unit at the Garda HQ in Wexford

Keith Sexton – a forensics officer

Frank Roche – a curious worker at the port of Rosslare

Eileen Roche – Frank Roche's wife who works part-time at a school

Daniel Roche – Frank and Eileen's son

Peter Booth – the manager at the port of Rosslare

Earl Defoe – a driver with a past and an interesting sideline

Leonard Walker – a mysterious man with some dubious connections

Inspector Ian Montgomery – a UK police officer

Superintendent Derek Harrington – a Garda superintendent from Dublin

Detective Inspector Jameson – a clumsy officer from Dublin

Garda Diarmuid Dillon – a Garda with a weak stomach

Aileen Brophy – the state pathologist

Dr Bukowski – a pathologist

Conor Grogan – a tech savvy member of An Garda Síochána

Michael Talbot – a neighbour of the Roches, who has a pet sheepdog

Kitty Malone – a school administrator

Avril Cunningham – a DS from Dublin's Fitzgibbon Street Garda station

Kevin Armstrong – an auditor

Chris Mulvaney – a senior Garda from Cork

If you enjoyed this book, please let others know by leaving a quick review on Amazon. Also, if you spot anything untoward in the paperback, get in touch. We strive for the best quality and appreciate reader feedback.

editor@thebookfolks.com

www.thebookfolks.com

Also in this series

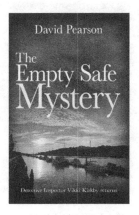

THE EMPTY SAFE MYSTERY (book 2)

When the manageress of a building society is found dead in her flat above the premises, Detective Inspector Vikki Kirkby is called in to investigate. With the safe open, and empty, the motive seems clear, but why such a brutal attack? The straight-talking detective will have to shake down the small southern Irish town of Wexford to get some answers.

Available before Christmas 2023.

More fiction by David Pearson

Head to the west coast of Ireland, or to its capital in the east…

FREE with Kindle Unlimited and available in paperback!

THE GALWAY HOMICIDES

Irish detective Maureen Lyons made a name for herself early in her career when quick thinking and sure footwork tripped up a robber and caught him red handed. She is now the life partner of Detective Mick Hays, team player and steady Eddie cop.

As these standalone murder mysteries progress, Maureen Lyons takes over much of the day-to-day policing of serious crime in Galway as Mick Hays rises in regional rank. Dynamic and courageous, Lyons does tend to take a few too many risks and that's a danger because far from being totally tranquil and peaceful, the west coast of Ireland throws up its fair share of bitter rivalries, simmering resentments, dodgy dealings, greed and outright nastiness that can lead to murder.

THE DUBLIN HOMICIDES SERIES

For Detective Inspector Aidan Burke, policing Dublin's streets is a duty, but protecting his officers comes first. That provides a good environment for promising detectives like DS Fiona Moore to grow. As this series of murder mysteries set in the metropolitan but at times parochial city and its surroundings progresses, we see Moore tackle difficult and dangerous cases with a good success rate. As Burke himself rises in rank, they become a formidable crime fighting duo.

Other titles of interest

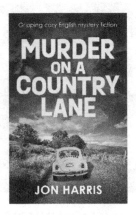

MURDER ON A COUNTRY LANE
by Jon Harris

After the shock of discovering a murder victim, young barmaid Julia isn't too perturbed because local garden centre owner Audrey White was a horrible so-and-so. But when her fingerprints are found all over a death threat, Julia becomes the police's prime suspect. Equipped with an unfetching ankle tag she must solve the crime to prove her innocence.

FREE with Kindle Unlimited and available in paperback!

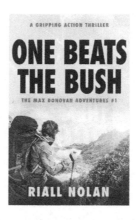

ONE BEATS THE BUSH
by Riall Nolan

Vietnam vet Max Donovan discovers his war-time buddy
has been accused of murder. Suspecting his friend has
been framed and unable to come up with the bail money,
he must solve the case himself. The feathers of a rare
bird were found near the crime scene, and Donovan
heads into the dangerous jungles of Papua New Guinea
and the shark-infested waters of the Coral Sea to discover
the truth.

FREE with Kindle Unlimited and available in paperback!

Sign up to our mailing list to find out about new releases, free books, special offers and more!

www.thebookfolks.com